LOVE, UNEXPECTED

Lighthouse Lovers
Book 5

SHANNON O'CONNOR

Copyright © 2025 Shannon O'Connor
All rights reserved.

All rights reserved. No part of this publication may be reproduced, distributed, or transmitted in any form or by any means, except in the case of brief quotations embodied in critical reviews and articles.

No use of AI was used to create this book, cover or edit any of the following. Please do NOT use my words, cover, or anything from this book in an AI form to feed AI.

Any resemblance to persons alive or dead is purely coincidental.

Cover by PagesandAdventures.

Edited by Victoria Ellis *Cruel Ink Editing & Design*.

Proofread by *Cruel Ink Editing & Design*.

Formatted by Shannon O'Connor.

❦ Created with Vellum

Love, Unexpected Playlist

Waterslide - John Legend

You're Not There - Lukas Graham

weak when ur around - blackbear

Ruin My Life - Zolita

Too Good To Be True - Rhys

Make You Mine - PUBLIC

Cool for the Summer - Demi Lovato

Foolish - Meghan Trainor

Say OK - Vanessa Hudgens

Better Version - FLETCHER

New Rules - Dua Lipa

Flowers - Miley Cyrus

Dirty Thoughts - Chloe Adams

Content Warnings

Please note some of these might be considered spoilers for parts of the story.

- Alcoholism
(On page descriptions of an alcoholic in recovery 5+ years)

- Negative Coming out Experience (disapproving parents)
(Past mentions)

ONE

Alana

I look around the ballroom of the hotel. The lights hanging above the altar, the candles at the end of every aisle, and the curtain hanging from the ceiling. Every detail I've hand-picked is perfect. I know I'm supposed to be upstairs, but I can't shake the feeling that something is wrong. If everything is perfect, then why doesn't it feel perfect? I've had this nagging feeling for months now. As much as I've tried to ignore it, I know I can't.

Maybe it is because my relationship with my fiancé has been shaky lately. It's far from what it used to be, and I don't know if it's possible to get back what we had. Will and I were happy in the beginning—happier than ever. But as more time passed, we grew complacent with each other. There is no desire, no fire, and definitely no passion. Don't I want that? I'd seen my parents' marriage. It was one of complacency, and although I'll be taken care of for the rest of my life, I don't think that's something I want anymore.

Will is perfect. On paper at least. He has a good job, wants the same things I want, and gets along well with my family. He's handsome, *okay* in bed, and he let me pick all the details for the wedding. But why does it feel like there is something off about us? Several of my friends have raised their concerns about him, but I've pushed them away. Sure, he didn't help out with the wedding, but he works more than I do. And maybe he isn't the best at taking care of me, but everyone has their strengths.

I look at my friends, who have all fallen in love this summer. Heather and Sage, Norah and Gemma, Wrenn and Ryleigh—even Kim and Zara. But I don't feel as happy as any of them. I'm not sure I ever did. It seems so natural for them. They don't have to work as hard as Will and I do. Most of them even fell in love when that was the last thing on their minds.

"Sweetheart? What are you doing down here? Shouldn't you be getting ready?" My mom catches me off guard. I wasn't supposed to let anyone see me before I was in my dress.

"I-I—" My words get stuck in my throat.

"Don't worry, I have everything taken care of. I'm double checking everything, so all you have to do is relax and get married today." My mother grabs my shoulders, and I force a smile.

"Thank you," I manage.

"Go, before someone sees you." She waves me away, but I don't budge.

"Did you know Daddy was the one?"

"What?" She's taken aback by the question. We don't talk about stuff like this.

"Was Daddy your first love? How did you know he was *the one*?"

"I, uh, no. He wasn't. I was actually seeing someone else. But your father caught my eye, and my parents approved, so that was that. Are you having cold feet or something?" She sounds worried, but I also know I can't tell her how I'm feeling.

"No, no. I'm fine," I lie.

"Okay good. You had me worried." She breathes a sigh of relief, and I bite the inside of my cheek.

I turn to go, sneaking out the back entrance of the hall so no one else will see me. I know I still have time before the guests start arriving, but I don't want to risk it. I don't know what I'm doing. I feel no better than I did twenty minutes ago. I can't keep running around, especially when I need to get my dress on and do my hair. My makeup is the only thing done. Maybe a mimosa and getting my hair done will calm me down. I make it back to the room, but as soon as I'm back in the chaos of the bridal suite, I start to panic. My sister is the first one to notice.

"What's going on? You look like you're either going to puke or pass out." Wrenn looks at me with an eyebrow raised.

"I just don't know if I can do this," I admit, and tears start flowing. Fuck, I'm going to ruin my makeup. I guess now I'll know if the mascara will hold up.

"Like the wedding or the marriage?" Wrenn asks.

"Both. All of it."

"Don't worry, you're just getting some pre-wedding jitters. They'll go away." Wrenn is holding a tissue for me when Heather walks back into the suite. Someone hands me a mimosa in a glass.

"I know I love him, but how am I supposed to be sure he's the one?" I cry.

"Can you tell her something encouraging? Were you nervous on your wedding day?" Ryleigh looks to Norah for help.

She shakes her head. "I wasn't nervous at all; I was sure about Finn."

The hair team comes in, ready to get back to work, and I can't handle this right now. I put down my glass of champagne and head out of the suite. Maybe I'm just having anxiety, and I need some air or something. I assume I'm alone until I hear Wrenn and Ryleigh approaching behind me.

"I'm fine," I lie.

They look at each other, knowing how much of a lie that is.

"You don't have to do this if you're not ready." Wrenn is the first to speak. I knew my sister would say something like that. She has made her stance on her future brother-in-law clear.

"What Wrenn means is, if you're feeling scared or nervous,

3

you can always postpone. People will understand," Ryleigh says lightly.

"I know neither of you like him. I just can't shake this feeling I'm having."

"It's not that we don't like him—" Ryleigh starts but Wrenn scoffs.

"Speak for yourself," Wrenn mumbles.

"We just think you aren't as happy as you could be." Ryleigh frowns.

"So you think I should just call the whole thing off? I can't do that." I turn away from them, not waiting for a reply.

"Alana, maybe just—"

"Look, just give me a few minutes to breathe. I'm going take a walk downstairs, and I'll be back soon. I just need some space to think." I press the button on the elevator, and it appears within seconds with a ding.

"Okay. We'll be back in the suite." Wrenn and Ryleigh take off, holding hands. And then something small hits me: when was the last time I held my fiancé's hand?

Sure, not everyone is a big fan of PDA. I learned that the hard way the many times I tried showing my affection. Especially this summer, when it caused a huge fight between Will and me. But holding hands is different than kissing in public. Don't I want someone who *wants* to hold my hand?

The more I look around, the more I realize what I have to do. I can't come back here, put on a face, and promise him forever. I can't do this. While I have my nerve, I sneak out the entrance of the hotel. I'm walking at full speed toward the entrance when I smack into something hard. Glancing in front of me, I see bright blue hair and a T-shirt that says, *I support women's rights and wrongs*. I quickly mumble an apology before racing out the front door of the hotel.

Only now comes the not-so-easy part. I left my phone and wallet upstairs, and there is no way I can go back in there undetected and get a chance like this again. If I'm going to do this...If

I am going to run out on my marriage, then I need to go however I can. So, I hop in the back of the first cab I see and rattle off Lovers, Maine. It

Lovers is the next town over, but now comes the tricky part; where should I go? I can't go home, that'll be the first place everyone looks. Besides, I share it with Will. I could go to my parents' house, but that's the next place everyone will look, and they might be the last people I want to face today. Then, I remember the last summer house on the estate. No one else is using it this summer because it's under renovations. But I know where we keep the hidden key, and we always keep each house stocked with supplies. It's the perfect hideout.

Thankfully, I convince the cab driver to drive me there and wait out front while I run inside and look for some money. We always used to keep some in the kitchen in case we needed a tip for deliveries, so I'm happy to find just enough for my fare plus a nice tip.

There's no one here, just like I anticipated. The key is hidden in the same spot it always is, tucked behind the mailbox with a piece of tape. It isn't like anyone is going to break in. Everyone knows everyone in this town. Thankfully, my parents will assume the motion on the Ring camera is just the handyman working. I look around the place and realize it's mostly covered in tools and those tarps people put down when they're working on something. I have no clue what renovations are being done here, but it's clear they're not done yet. Hopefully I'll at least have tonight to be alone.

I scrounge through the cabinets for something quick to eat before retreating to a bedroom. I choose the one I used to stay in as a kid and lock the door behind me. I don't have any way of communicating with anyone, which makes me feel oddly free—and then the tears start falling. I climb into bed and pull the covers over myself. I know I should probably take off my makeup, but I don't have any energy. All I want to do is cry and sleep and forget about this mess of a day. There's only so much time until someone comes looking for me. Then I'll be bombarded by questions and accusations. I twist the diamond ring on my left hand and stare at it. It once brought me so much joy looking at it, but now it's just a reminder of what I left behind. I know this isn't a mistake and that this is the right choice for me...

I just hope everyone else will see it that way.

TWO

Harmony

I put down my vape when I see Millie racing around the corner from the bathroom. She is in eyesight while I step outside for a hit. I make a point not to hit it in front of her. She's only six and doesn't need to be breathing it in. Not that I need to be either, but I've been using it for so long, it's more of a habit than I care to admit. Millie runs over to me with her pink tutu skirt flowing in the air. I love that she dresses like herself. She's wearing a T-shirt that says, *snacks are my love language*. I'm pretty sure she got wearing silly T-shirts from me and the girly aspect from her other mom.

"Is someone getting married here?" Millie asks as we pass by a room with wedding decorations.

"I think so." I glance inside but it doesn't look like anyone's in there yet.

"Can we watch!? I bet it's going to be so pretty! I wanna see the bride's dress!" Millie gasps.

"I don't think we can just sneak into someone's wedding, Mills."

"Ah man." She frowns.

"Maybe we'll see the bride coming down before she goes in."

"Ooh okay!" She nods happily.

I'm not thrilled to be working on my day with Millie, but she is sort of used to it. I'm always called in for odd jobs and they pay well, so it isn't like I can afford to turn them down. My ex-wife and I have joint custody, and no one is paying the other child support as long as we can both afford what Millie needs. So I take every job I can to make sure I won't be scraping by. I'd rather have money in my savings than not enough.

"I just have to fix the window frame in this room next door and then we can head home," I tell her.

"Okay!" Millie dances around the room. I've given her one of my old phones to use as an iPod, so she hooks it up to play music while she dances.

The window is in one of the larger conference rooms, and without all the chairs and tables set up, there's a lot of room for dancing. I focus on what I'm doing so we can get out of here faster. Millie is almost seven, so she isn't getting into trouble or in that phase of running away anymore. Thank goodness. I do not miss that. So I know as long as I hear her dancing and singing behind me, she's okay.

I pick up the new window frame and remove all the plastic and cardboard. The other window is already removed, and there's hot air blowing in from outside. Summer is officially over but no one has told the weather. I can't imagine getting married on a day like today, but then again, I doubt I will ever get married again. I love Millie, but her mother and I were once best friends who rushed into marriage and kids way too early. Now we barely speak unless it's about Millie. It's better that way.

I slide the window into the frame and secure it. I glance back at Millie, who's still dancing, and smile. To be young and that carefree again. Once I'm sure the window is all set, I start cleaning up my tools. I hear Millie running over to the door, and I see her peeking her head out.

"What's going on?" I ask.

"Shh!" She shushes me, and I laugh. She's just as nosey as her mother.

"Don't be spying on people." I laugh.

Picking up the toolbox, I clean up the small mess I made and toss it in the trashcan next to the door. Then I peek outside the door over Millie's head and realize she's spying on the wedding party. There are several women dressed in bridesmaids' dresses talking to an older woman who looks anything but happy. For some reason, she looks super familiar to me, but I can't quite place where I know her from. Then again, Lovers is a small town. Maybe I've seen her at the market or something.

I pull Millie back inside and ask quietly, "What's going on?"

"They can't find the bride," she says with wide eyes.

A runaway bride? Holy shit. Millie looks at me anxiously, and I nod, letting her go back to spying. Truthfully, I'm curious and it isn't like we can walk past them without interrupting their conversation.

"What do you mean you can't find her?!" the older woman shouts.

"Well, she went for a walk and never came back," a woman with dark purple hair says.

"Wrenn, this is not the time for one of your games. I swear, if you're just messing with me, I will have your head," the older woman snaps.

"Mom, I swear. Can someone else please confirm I'm not lying since my mother thinks this is my idea of a joke?" The purple-haired woman scoffs.

"It's true, Mrs. Thomas, we haven't been able to find her. She was quite upset about the wedding and getting married. Truthfully, I think she was having cold feet," a redhead says.

"Cold feet?" A man joins the conversation now. Judging by his tux, I'd assume he's the groom.

"Will, don't stress. I'm sure we'll find her." The older woman puts a hand on his chest in an attempt to calm him.

"You can't find her?!" he yells.

Everyone goes silent, and he turns red with rage. "Where the hell is she? I can't put up with her dramatics right now. It's our freaking wedding day. Isn't she going to grow up?"

The purple-haired woman balls her fists, and a brunette holds her back when she steps forward like she's going to punch him. They step back and disappear down a hallway, I assume to calm down.

"This is all your fault!" The groom turns to another brunette.

"Excuse me?" Her jaw drops.

"You filled her head with all that crap. She was perfectly content with us and how things were until you two talked after her bachelorette party," he yells.

"Content? Maybe your bride-to-be didn't want to be content the rest of her life and she actually wanted to be happy. All I told her was the truth, and I stand by it now more than ever. She deserves better than you, and if she ran away, I hope it's because she came to her senses." The brunette stands tall against the groom.

"Okay, this isn't helping. Start looking for her, and I'll attempt to stall everyone else," the older woman steps in.

The bridesmaids disperse, and the groom scoffs. Everyone clears the hall, and I take it as an opportunity for Millie and me to get out of here.

"But I don't wanna go!" She groans.

"We're done, let's get home," I tell her.

Begrudgingly, she follows me to the car. We see some of the bridesmaids outside looking for the bride, but I don't see her around. Not that we'd know what she looked like anyway. I assume she isn't running away in her wedding dress. I put Millie into her car seat and buckle her in. She picks up her lunchbox and pulls out a bag of goldfish.

I text my boss that I got the window done and send the photos I took as proof. I don't need to send them, but it's easier to show proof then have anyone question me. I click in the location of the apartment into my GPS app. I'm still not used to this small town, having only moved here last month. Millie's other mom, Jamie, got a new job in Lovers, and since I can work from anywhere, I agreed to move from Chicago to Maine. She also wanted to be a bit closer to family, which is something I can understand. It's a bit of a jolt from big city to small town, but there's enough work to keep me busy. Plus, I wouldn't have let Jamie and Millie move so far away without me. I got an apartment rather quickly, and even though I'm not fully unpacked yet, the essentials are.

"Are you excited to start school on Monday?" I ask, looking in the rearview mirror at Millie.

"Sort of." She frowns.

"What's going through your head?"

"Well, I'm just worried I won't know anyone, and what if everyone has friends already?" She sighs.

"Second grade is a hard time to start somewhere new. But I think if anyone can do it, it's you. You'll just introduce yourself to people until you find friends you want to stick with."

"You think I'll find some?"

"I do. It's a smaller town so I think people will be excited to have a new friend to play with."

Mille nods with a smile. I won't say it out loud, but I'm worried about the same things for her. It's hard enough being the new kid in a school, but starting in second grade when everyone is paired up? I hope everyone will be kind to her. She has a soft and artistic soul that I don't want dimmed.

"Mama?" Millie pulls me from my thoughts.

"What's up, Mills?"

"Do you think we can go to the park tomorrow?"

I laugh. She's already moved on to something new. "Of course we can."

Millie starts rattling off about all the things she wants to do. The park is just outside the elementary school, so maybe we'll run into someone who will be in her class. Jamie and I will be splitting the week with her, picking her up and dropping her off at school on different days. It'll be a bit of a different schedule than we had in Chicago, but I'm grateful for more time with her.

Most of my week consists of working on the Thomas estate. I'm renovating the kitchen and adding another bathroom to the place. It's a big job that's going to take a lot of time over the next month. I don't mind, really, because I'll be alone. It seems to be a bonus summer home of sorts for the Thomas family, and as far as I know, no one is living there. It makes doing my job even easier. Too often, an extra-helpful dad will try to help, or a lonely housewife will hit on me. Neither of which I like to get involved with. It's much easier when I can go in, get the job done, and leave. They were very clear about what they wanted, and if I have any questions, I should email Mr. Thomas. He's taking care of the bill and most of the issues, the only thing his wife cares about is the design. She's almost done picking the tiles for everything, and then the painters and designers will fix everything else.

Now that I think about it, I need to stop by there tomorrow night. I drop Millie off at her mom's so she can take her for the first day of school. Then I need to swing by and measure a few things for the Thomas house. If I don't need to drag Millie over there, I won't. It's a mess from all the tarps and current projects.

I'm a bit all over the place when I have the place to myself. I start a project and work on it until I'm bored or run out of materials, then move on to the next one and then go back when I feel like it. There is no timeline for specific tasks, so it works for me. It's also a great way for me to get my stress out.

THREE

Alana

When I wake up, I have no clue what time it is. None of the windows are open, and there's no clock in this room. After a quick trip to the bathroom, I find a clock in the living room with the time. It's almost five p.m. How the hell did I sleep for almost twenty-four hours? I woke up a few times to pee, drink water, and cry. But I really slept that long? I stretch—my bones feel achy without my morning yoga and run. Thankfully, I find an old pair of glasses in the bedside table. They aren't perfect, but I can at least see with them. I had to pop out my contacts before bed last night, and it isn't like I brought extras.

Looking around the room, I grab a handful of cereal for breakfast and then lie on the couch. I'm about to turn on the TV when I see an iPad on the bottom shelf of the coffee table. It's my sister's old one from college, so who knows if it even works. I scrounge around the house for a charger, finding one in the bigger bedroom and leaving it on the counter to charge. Within five minutes, it turns on automatically, and I'm grateful my sister doesn't have a password. I decide to log into my iCloud and see if anyone is looking for me. I assume they are, and I shouldn't let everyone worry.

As soon as I login, more than three dozen messages and missed calls pop up. All my friends and family are asking where the hell I am and if I'm okay. Will has texted a few times, too, but never called. I'm too nervous to click on his messages, and I'm not sure I want to see what he wrote. I'm about to figure out who I should call first when the iPad starts ringing. It slips from my hands, and I drop it on the counter. Gemma is calling. Does she know I turned on my iCloud? Taking a deep breath, I answer, bracing myself.

"Thank fuck. Norah! She answered!" Gemma calls as soon as she sees me. Glancing at the little box in the corner, I realize I look like a freaking mess.

"Hi," I say meekly.

"Are you okay? Where are you?" Gemma asks, and Norah sits on the couch next to her.

"I-I'm okay."

"Alana, are you sure? No one knows where you've been the last twenty-four hours," Norah says softly.

"I've been sleeping." It isn't a lie.

"Jesus Christ. I'm going to kick your ass. Tell me you're somewhere safe." Gemma sighs.

"I am." I nod.

"Do you want us to come get you? We don't have to tell anyone, if that's what you're afraid of. But everyone is so worried," Gemma says.

"No. I-I don't think I'm ready to be around people yet," I admit.

"Alana, we have to tell everyone we found you. Your mom was threatening to call the police. She's convinced you were kidnapped."

"You can tell them I'm okay, but I don't want to talk to anyone. I'm not ready to come back."

"Okay." Norah nods.

"How did you know to call me?"

"I have your phone. It popped up that you logged into your iCloud. I can't see your location, but I figured if you logged in, you might pick up," Gemma explains.

"Ah." I nod.

"I'll keep it on. But promise me you'll pick up if we call here? It was terrifying not knowing where you went," Gemma says, and Norah nods in agreement.

"Yeah, okay." It's fair enough. They aren't demanding to come find me, they're just concerned.

"Do you need anything? Clothes? Food?" Norah offers.

"Not yet." My mother kept some of her summer wardrobe here, and I know there's food.

"Okay. I'm going to give everyone else a call. But please stay safe."

"I will. I promise."

We hang up, and I feel a tiny bit better now that I know everyone won't be worrying about me. And I'm relieved Gemma and Norah aren't pushing to know my location. I lie backward on the couch and put a pillow over my face. I scream into it twice, even though in reality, I could probably scream without it on and no one would hear me.

Upon thinking that, I hear the lock to the front door click open. I jolt up, sitting on the couch. The pillow falls to my lap. The door begins to open, and I jump up to find something to use as a weapon. The only things nearby are my sneaker and a pillow. I opt for the sneaker and hold it above my head, racing toward the intruder. They walk in, holding a toolbox that they drop the second they see me.

"What the fuck!?" they yell. The toolbox hits the floor with a clang, and their eyes widen.

"Who are you?" we both yell at the same time.

"I'm a contractor! A handywoman. I work here. Who are you?" I put down my shoe and eye the woman. Her bright blue cropped hair and the T-shirt that reads, *Eat Pussy, it's Vegan.*

"I-I. This is my family's house."

"And you are?" She doesn't relax until I say my name.

"I'm Alana Thomas."

"Do you have any way to prove it?" She eyes me.

"Uh, actually I don't." I frown. I ran away without ID or my phone or anything tying me to being me.

"How do I know you're not an intruder who, like, read their mail or something?"

"How do I know you're really a contractor?" I counter.

She slips her hand in her front pocket and holds out a business card.

Handywoman Harmony
For all your contracting needs

"Oh." I relax.

"I really have to call the owners about this," she says, reaching for her phone.

"No!" I yell. "Look, my parents don't know I'm here. I *am* Alana Thomas, but the reason I have no way to prove that is because I ran away from my wedding yesterday. I knew where the key was, and I'm hiding out. So please don't call them."

"Do you know your father's phone number?"

"What?"

"Look, I won't call them, but I need some way to prove you're you. Do you know your father's number? I assume you'd know if you are who you say you are."

I relax. "Yes, his work or his cell? I assume he gave you his work, but I can tell you both." I rattle off the numbers as she checks against the one in her phone.

"Okay. I can come back then, but I do have to work here.

Especially if you aren't telling them you're here, I can't afford to get fired if they think I'm not working," Harmony explains.

"I understand. I'll stay out of your way as long as you keep my location to yourself."

"Deal." Harmony picks up her toolbox and steps by me cautiously. I don't blame her; I did threaten her with a shoe.

I retreat to the bedroom and decide a shower is in order. First, I look through my parents closet and pull out some clothes to wear. Then I head to the bathroom. I almost scream when I see how caked on my makeup is. I look like I went for a run in the rain with a full face. No wonder Harmony was looking at me like that; I look like a crazy person. I try scrubbing off the makeup but decide it's easier to do everything in the shower.

Once I'm sure my face is clean, I get to work on my hair. There's so much hairspray and a billion knots to untangle. Thank goodness my mother likes the best bath products, or I'd be tempted to cut my hair off. Although that might truly mean I'm having a manic episode. Running away from your wedding is one thing, but cutting off almost a foot of hair might be too far. I manage to fix it before giving up.

I change into my mother's clothes, which are a little big on me, but they do the trick. I pull my hair into a tight bun and decide to see if Harmony is still here. I can hear her working in the kitchen, so I head back to my bedroom and lie in bed. There isn't much for me to do in here, but I don't want to disturb her.

I stare at the ceiling and hope that she really can keep a secret for me. If worst comes to worst, she tells my parents, and then I have to deal with the downfall of talking to them. Knowing how much I disappointed them and how I disappeared without another word, I bet they are furious with me. They loved Will, and they were happy I was getting married. It was all we talked about for the last year. But it was clear that they had expectations for me as much as Will did. Everything was always being given and shown to me about how my life would be. Besides running away, I can't remember the last time I made a choice for myself.

Even the idea of having a big wedding was something Will and my mother cooked up. They thought the optics would be better if we had a bigger wedding. No one cared about what I wanted.

I sigh. I love my mother, she was hard on my sister, but she meant well. I just know I'm not ready to face her yet. That disapproving tone and asking me what I'm going to do now. I feel like everything I had planned for the next five years was for other people and not myself. Now that I have the opportunity to choose my own future, I feel overwhelmed but also excited.

I know I can't live here forever. I mean, eventually I need to get back to work and talk to everyone and be a person in the world again. But I'm not ready yet. I need more time to figure out whatever my next step is. And at least for the next few days, my next step is to recalibrate. I've been on go-mode for months now, and I need a break. I finally feel all of the tension in my body as I let go of the future I planned. It's probably why I cried for hours, and why I feel the urge to cry again. I've never been good at expressing my emotions like Wrenn, always keeping things inside until they ultimately burst. But I want to feel this so I can get past it.

I'll forever be a woman who ran away from her own wedding. I'm a runaway bride. It isn't something I can take back or undo. The label sticks to me like glue. Still, no part of me regrets it. I'm sad and exhausted, but I know it was the right choice. If I was on my honeymoon with Will right now, I'd only be married and unhappy. That's no way to start a marriage. Maybe I'll never marry, but at least I know I didn't settle for something—and someone—I don't truly want.

Tears fall down my cheeks, and I rub them with the sleeves of my shirt. I wish I had someone here that could understand what I'm going through. My friends are probably all relieved I'm not spending the rest of my life with Will. They had said it gracefully, voicing their concerns, and when I shut them all down, they stopped. God, how silly do I feel about that now? They smiled and said as long as I was happy, they'd support me. I wonder if they're sighing a breath of relief now, knowing they won't have to fake it during holidays and birthdays. That's kind of how I feel. It's hard to explain how I feel relief while also being sad. Two contradicting emotions at the same time feel weird.

Maybe, hopefully, this too will pass.

FOUR

Harmony

Now that Alana and I are past her wanting to hit me with a shoe, I'm able to get to work. I mainly need to get some measurements, but I also need to do a little touch up on something in the kitchen. It's weird knowing she's in the house, but I relax a bit when I hear the shower running. I take a hit from my vape and slide it back into my pocket. After the initial shock wore off, I realized I recognize her. I saw her yesterday at the hotel, when she ran into me. *Literally*. She didn't stop to say anything more than a mumbled apology, but I wouldn't forget that ass. I had been waiting for Millie to go to the bathroom, and she was on her way out. I had no idea that was the runaway bride everyone was looking for.

I understand why she doesn't want anyone to know where she is. I'm sure running away from a wedding isn't an easy decision, and she probably needs some time to get past things before she heads home. I just don't want to get caught with her here if she isn't who she says she is. After a quick Instagram search, I also connected her to her profile. The last post was only a few days ago—with her wedding nails and engagement ring. I wonder what happened to make her go from an excited bride to a runaway one. God, I'm hanging out with Millie too much. She's making me as nosey as she is.

Speaking of Millie, I check my phone again. I know there won't be any new messages from Jamie, but I always worry when Millie isn't with me. Especially when I have power tools on and could possibly miss the call or text.

Alana comes out of her room with a clean face and new clothes. I'm not going to say anything when she's standing there with a face of makeup down her cheeks. My guess is, a night of crying would do that to someone. Now that she is bare-faced, I take a better look at her. Her dark hair is pulled into a bun on her head, instead of the disarray it was in before. Her eyes are more golden-brown than dark brown, and she has almost a perfectly symmetrical face. She is really beautiful. I take another hit of my vape and try not to think about that.

"Do you do that a lot in here?" Alana wrinkles her nose.

"Excuse me?"

"I just...I really hate the smell of vapes, and I actually care about my lungs."

I feign a laugh. "There are about a billion worse things for your lungs. Especially when I'm renovating this place."

Alana frowns. Her red lips purse, but I sigh. It's technically her house after all.

"I'll be sure to go outside to vape," I assure her.

"Thank you." She hesitates before looking around.

"You're welcome to be out here. It might get noisy, but you don't have to be stuck in a bedroom the whole time I'm here. I just can't have you in the way for safety reasons," I explain.

"Okay." She nods.

Alana makes a spot for herself on the couch and picks up a book off the coffee table. I don't know if she's actually reading it because it seems like she's just flipping through the pages. I try to focus on my work but it's a little hard when I can feel her eyes on me. Maybe I'd be better off coming back in the morning. I usually get here around eight, but since she's here, I'll have to check what time is okay. I'm sure she doesn't want to wake up to the sounds of drilling and sanding. I start to pack up my stuff. Most of it stays here, but I grab the stuff I need to take with me. I got all the measurements I need so I can always catch up on everything else tomorrow.

"I'm going to head out. But I'll be back tomorrow, and I'll be sure to knock," I tell Alana.

"Okay, thank you." She smiles softly. It's the first time I've really seen her smile, and it doesn't look genuine.

"Is ten a.m. okay?"

"Yeah, don't worry about me."

"Do you…umm need anything? I know you're sort of hiding out, but you have supplies?" I don't really know what she might need but it feels weird leaving her here to hide out.

"I'm okay. There's food and I have AC, so I'm set."

"Okay. See you tomorrow."

I walk to my car, and as soon as I put down my tools, I take a heavy puff of my vape. At least she wasn't telling me I couldn't smoke it at all. My ex had a problem with the smell too. But it helps me keep my drinking under control. Although, I've been sober for almost five years now, so I could probably quit my vape and be okay. I've just never had a reason to. They say when you quit drinking, you often pick up other habits to replace the one you lost. I didn't think much of it until I started vaping. Cigarette smoke has always been too harsh for me, and drugs seem like the wrong way to go, but vaping is okay.

I pull out my phone as I get in the car and check my messages again. Jamie messaged to let me know Millie wants to FaceTime before bed tonight. I smile. It isn't the same as seeing her in person, but I love her little face on my phone. I drive home and the second I get inside, I click on the FaceTime button. It rings for a moment before Millie's face appears.

"Hi Mama!" Her smile is the size of her face.

"Hi Mills, how's my girl doing?"

"Great! Mommy helped me pick out my first day of school outfit. Wanna see?" she asks excitedly.

"Of course."

Millie races across her bedroom to bring over a hanger with a pink unicorn dress. "Mommy says I have to wear shorts under it, so I don't show my underwear when I'm doing the monkey bars."

"Your mom is right, but that dress is cute. You'll look awesome." I smile.

"Thanks! I'm excited for tomorrow. Still nervous, too, but it'll probably be fine. Right?"

"Yes, it will. And you can call to tell me all about it tomorrow, okay?"

"Yes! Mommy said you have work tomorrow but I'll see you this weekend, right?"

"Of course. I may stop by one day after work. I just gotta check my schedule with Mom's," I explain.

"Yay! I can't wait." She smiles.

"I know it's late, so I'll let you get ready for bed. I can't wait to hear about how your first day went."

"Okay Mama! I love you." She blows me a kiss.

"I love you too."

We hang up and I sigh. It's hard to see her on the nights I don't have her. It's like a part of me wishes Jamie and I could've worked it out, if only because then I'd have Millie all the time. I don't say this out loud. It wouldn't change anything. We're divorced for a reason, and for a divorced couple, we do get along pretty well. I just miss my girl.

I hate to admit it but I'm also a little lonely lately. Jamie and I had this whole life in Chicago. It's where her parents and our friends are. But now that we moved, I barely have the time to make new friends. I could call one of my old friends, but it's not like I can see them. It's also hard to make friends as a grown woman. No one prepared me for that. Especially considering I basically work on my own. It isn't like I'm befriending my clients. So where am I supposed to meet people my age?

Jamie enjoys going to bars and meeting people with similar interests. I think she's going to a paint and sip with other moms. But I need a sober event. The problem is, most things these days are paired with alcohol. A book club, a cooking class, even the PTA meetings in Chicago—Jamie had to go to because the moms started serving wine. It feels nearly impossible to find something people can do sober. Why is drinking so normalized?

FIVE

Alana

The next morning, I make sure to have my alarm set for nine a.m. so I can be ready when Harmony gets here. I shower since I cried more tears than I care to admit, and I want to feel semi-human. I snack on a granola bar and wish I had something good to eat, but it isn't like I have my car or can order takeout without someone recognizing me. I manage to find some workout gear of my mom's and decide that, once Harmony gets here, I'll go for a run. It used to be part of my morning routine, and I've been missing it. Maybe it will help me feel like myself again. And at least I can force myself to go outside today. The houses are so far from each other, it isn't like anyone will see me running along the path. At 10:01, Harmony knocks on the door, and I'm there to let her in.

"Morning. Going somewhere?" Harmony asks as I put on my sneakers.

"Just taking a quick run around the property. I have a key so if you need to go out, you can lock it."

"Gotcha. Well, I grabbed you a coffee, so it'll be here when you get back."

"You got me a coffee?" I ask, surprised.

"Yeah, I don't know what you like, but you strike me as

someone who enjoys strong coffee, so I got it black and brought sugar and milk in case you don't."

"Thank you." I smile. "I do drink it black."

"Cool. I'll put it on the counter. Have a nice run." Harmony lets herself inside, and I head outside.

It's brighter than I anticipated, and I wish I had my sunglasses, but those are somewhere in my luggage. I run down the path toward the next property and keep an easy pace. I don't want to do too much on the first day. Or land myself in the hospital. Too much gossip would be had.

I keep pace and run the perimeter of the house. I can see the water over the hill and the beach is basically empty today. I think it's a Monday or Tuesday which means all the lifeguards are gone for the summer. School starts in town this week, so most people will be busy during the day. I keep jogging until I reach the front of the house again. I wish I had my Apple watch, then I'd know how far I ran and the pace. I decide to do another lap around the house, starting with the path on the road in front of the house. As I'm running, I hear a car coming. It's probably someone lost, since that happens a lot. But I don't want anyone to see me, so I try to run out of the way.

"Alana! Alana is that you?!" an unfamiliar voice calls out from the car.

There's no use, I can't run back to the house fast enough. I turn around and jog closer to the car. When I get close enough to see an array of blonde curls, I realize it's just Maeve—Heather's girlfriend's best friend. She's staying in the house with Heather. Her apartment building caught on fire a few weeks ago, and I let her stay until she got back on her feet.

"Hey, Maeve." I don't know her that well, but she was at the wedding.

"Are you okay?" Maeve parks the car but is still talking through the open passenger window.

"I'm great." I force a smile.

"Well, that's bullshit. But do you need anything? You're not running from someone are you?" She looks back as if someone is going to appear.

"No, just running to destress."

"Got it."

"Listen, do you think you could—"

"I won't tell anyone I saw you." She smiles.

I blow a breath of relief. "Thank you."

"I know I'm basically a friend of a friend, but if you want someone to talk to, I'm a pretty good listener. And I won't bill you," she jokes. Then it registers that she just graduated with her social work degree, and she's using it to be a therapist.

"I'm okay."

"You're not. And that's okay. Just let me know if that changes or you need anything. I can bring over food, clothes, whatever. I won't mention it to anyone."

I hesitate before answering. This could be the answer to my prayers. Maeve has no reason to tell anyone she's seen me. Maybe I could ask her to bring me some things and keep hanging out here. I can only survive on granola bars and cereal with no milk for so long.

"I-I don't have a phone."

"Do you need one?"

"I don't really want one. I just have no way of contacting you." I don't think I have her number in the iPad.

"Why don't you tell me what you need, I'll write it all down and bring it over tonight. Then I can check in every few days while you're here," she suggests.

"You'd do that?"

"You gave me a free place to live when mine burnt down. I think the least I can do is keep your secret and bring you supplies."

"I'm just not ready to face anyone yet." I sigh.

"Here, let me park in the driveway and we can chat."

I nod and follow her car along the path. She parks next to

Harmony's car and steps out. She's actually my height, which surprises me, because most of my friends aren't as tall as I am.

"Your friends just wanted to know you're safe. And now that they know that, they aren't looking for you. Your parents and your ex-fiancé might be, but as far as the girls go, they respect your privacy. That said, I only know what Heather and Sage tell me. Which isn't much. But even if I did tell them I knew where you were and I was bringing you things, they wouldn't ask where you are. I think you know that," Maeve explains.

I nod. I know my friends will be okay now that they've spoken to me. "I figured as much. They're not the ones I'm worried about facing."

"I get that. So, you tell me what you might need, and I'll see what I can do." Maeve smiles.

"I would love some food. I don't have any allergies, and I can cook, so even if you just bring ingredients, I can make my own stuff. I don't know if you can get my clothes, you might have to talk to my sister to get them. If you do and they want to give you my phone, that's fine. I won't promise I'm turning it on and using it yet. But it wouldn't hurt to have it for an emergency."

"Okay. That I can do." She pauses. "Is this your car?"

"No, the contractor is here doing work on the house."

"Are you okay with them here?" She raises an eyebrow.

"She's nice. Harmless, she brought me coffee and asked the same things you did."

"Okay. I'll see if I can get all this by tonight, if not I'll be here tomorrow."

"Sounds great to me. Thank you, Maeve. I really appreciate it." I smile.

"I know what it's like to feel like you're starting your life over. I know it may not be the same, but in a way, you lost a lot of the same things I did. So if you ever feel like talking, just let me know." She offers a half smile, and I nod.

I'm honestly not against talking to her—or another therapist.

I'm just not ready for that yet. There's too much going through my mind that I'm not ready to admit out loud yet.

"Thank you," is all I manage before she leaves.

Feeling exhausted from human interaction, I decide to head inside. I can shower and then enjoy a fresh cup of coffee. I kick my sneakers to the side neatly and go to find Harmony so she knows I'm in the house. I turn around the corner of the kitchen and find her in the backyard cutting wood. She lifts her shirt halfway to expose a set of tattooed abs. They glisten with sweat in the sunlight, and I drop my jaw. Holy shit. She wipes her brow with the bottom of her shirt before noticing me.

"Oh hey, how was your run?" she asks.

I quickly pick up my jaw and mumble out a response. "It was good. Just wanted to tell you I'm back."

"Sounds good." She nods and takes a swig from a reusable water bottle covered in stickers. She must notice me staring because she adds, "My daughter did this. I tried to explain unicorns aren't professional, but she's six."

"You have a daughter?" I don't know why I'm surprised. Almost half my friends are gay and either have or want kids.

"I do. Millie. She's with my ex-wife during the week and with me on the weekends," she explains.

"Ah." Ex-wife. I don't know why that triggers a weird feeling to erupt in my stomach.

Harmony goes back to sawing the wood in half, sliding on safety googles first and then turning on the saw. She looks like something out of an old porno with her sleeveless tank top showing off her tattooed arms and her tight jeans with her work belt on. A shiver runs down my spine, and I excuse myself to the bathroom.

I look in the mirror and notice my cheeks are red and flushed. That has to be because of my run, right? It hasn't been that long since I've had sex. It's been awhile since I've had an orgasm, though. For far too long, I've secretly been getting off in the shower or when Will was at work. He'd never managed to make me come, and even though I've never faked it, he didn't seem much interested in trying, either. I tried introducing toys and using them when I was alone, and he'd tell me that felt like I was cheating on him. I knew it was bullshit, so I was a secret masturbator—even in my own home.

Ugh. The more things like that pop up, I can't believe I didn't see it before. Why the hell had I let it go on until our wedding day? Why didn't I stop it before then? Instead of pondering that, I decide to do a little self-care. I turn on the shower, thankful the shower head is detachable, and undress. Harmony is all the way in the backyard and has the saw on, so it isn't like she'd be able to hear me.

I play with my breasts first, squeezing and pinching my nipples. They were already hard to start, probably from lack of touch. What's most surprising is when I slide my hand down to my pussy, I'm already soaked. My fingers glide through the wetness, and I let out a moan. I close my eyes and lean back on the cool tile of the shower wall. A shiver runs through me as I brush across my clit.

"Oh!" My lips try to hold back my moans, but I'm so turned on.

I pick up the shower head and let the cool water hit my clit. I switch the settings from rainfall to jet and gasp. It's a little intense at first, until it starts to hit my clit perfectly. Fuck. The image of Harmony's abs pop into my head, and I groan. Her perfectly tattooed arms and the way I want to run my hands through her short blue hair.

"Yes! Yes!" I moan as the orgasm hits.

I let my brain run wild with thoughts about Harmony. I've had fantasies about women before—it's nothing new. Women are easier to fantasize about than a grunting and hairy man. Women are soft and smooth, and I know they'd be able to find the clit.

SIX

Harmony

My weekly AA meetings are on Wednesday mornings. I like that it splits up the week, reminding me to keep going with the program. It's different than my old meeting back in Chicago—less people for starters. But I appreciate that I have somewhere to go. I wouldn't be much without my meetings to hold me accountable.

I wasn't much of a talker at first. I went and listened, I stayed sober, but it took me a long time to actually have the courage to stand up and share my story. My sponsor, Ruby, had a lot to do with that. She's queer, has been sober for over twenty years, and she always calls me on my bullshit. I often tell her how much I owe her my life. We still talk on the phone, which helps on the days when I want a drink. I'm mostly past those, but every once in a while, they sneak up on me.

"Today we have someone receiving their five-year chip. Harmony, come on up here!" Mr. Reid claps, and I stand up from the squeaky folding chair. He hands me my five-year chip, and I shake his hand.

"This is probably where I'm supposed to say, once you hit five years, it gets easier. But that's a bold-faced lie. Every day is hard when you're sober. Sometimes I think about drinking, and it's like a fantasy. But every day I remember the reality, that I'm not someone who can have just one drink, or just one sip, and be okay. I remind myself of the pain I caused when I was drinking and how much I don't want to go back to that. And I remind myself that I'm not only doing this for me, but also for my daughter, who looks up to me." I grip the podium as I think of her.

"The first two years of her life are a blur for me, and I'll always regret not getting to have those memories. But I do want to thank Ruby for being my sponsor and kicking my ass to meetings in the beginning. I wouldn't be here today without her. I hope for another five years with her as my sponsor." I thank her even though she's not here, because I know she's be proud of me.

I sit back down, with my new chip in hand, and Mr. Reid closes the meeting for us. We mingle for a bit with the terrible coffee Mrs. Greer always burns and stale donuts I think someone gets for free from the bakery in town. Then we all close up the folding chairs and put them away. The church basement is free for our meetings as long as we clean up after. I help Mr. Reid clean up since I have time before I need to be at Jamie's house.

"Good meeting today, eh?" Mr. Reid always says this. I think he's just happy when people come.

"Yes." I smile.

"Congrats on five years. It's no small feat; it takes forever to earn and a second to lose." He winks.

"I hear you're coming up on an anniversary soon, right?"

"Yes, almost twenty-five years. I have another fifty-two days." He chuckles.

One thing I've noticed, is that every alcoholic can tell you exactly when their last drink was. It's not something you forget, and we often count how many days until our next anniversary. I think it gives us something positive to look forward to.

"One day."

We both head our separate ways, and I head to Jamie's house.

Today was a half day for Millie, and despite Jamie working from home, she asked if I could take her for the rest of the day. She's understanding of my meeting, so I show up right on schedule. Millie runs outside to hug me as I get out of the car.

"Mama!" She slams against my body, and I smile.

"Hey, Mills." I kiss the top of her head.

"Mommy's making me lunch, and then we can go!" she says excitedly.

I follow her inside and slide off my shoes by the door. Jamie hates dirt in the house—something that used to be inevitable for us since she had a contractor for a wife.

"Hey, Jamie," I call out, warning her I'm coming in.

We're the sort of exes who get along. We're not *friends*, but we get along. Especially in front of Millie. She saw enough of us fighting throughout the period before our divorce, so we make a point not to fight like that anymore.

"Hey, Har. I'm just making her some lunch. Your meeting go okay?" Jamie pushes back her dark curls.

"Five years today." I pop the chip on the counter, and she looks at it.

"Wow. You must feel amazing," she praises.

"I do."

We don't talk about it anymore, neither one of us wanting to rehash the past. But a lot of what led to our divorce was my drinking. I'd drink, we'd fight, and it would be chaos. It wasn't until she begged me to get help that I realized how bad we were. I tried my best to get sober on my own, but Jamie couldn't wait around to see if it would work. She took Millie and told me I couldn't see her until I was sober for longer than a week. It absolutely killed me, but it was the only thing that kicked my ass into shape. I've apologized many times since about how my drinking affected her, and I think she's since forgiven me. But I also know we're never going to go back to what we used to be. You can't undo the past; sometimes you just have to move forward.

"Mills has school tomorrow at eight. You can walk her to the front doors, and she finds her classroom. Make sure she has money for lunch, since she doesn't like to bring anything. Oh, and she did her homework already," Jamie says, switching into mom-mode.

"Homework? She's in first grade."

"She had a math worksheet and needed to read a chapter of her book. The math she didn't mind, the book was like pulling teeth." Jamie grimaces.

"That sounds like me." I chuckle.

"Exactly what I told her." Jamie shakes her head. "Millie! Come eat!" Millie comes running and jumps onto the chair at the counter. She takes a bite of her sandwich and does a little wiggle, as if she's dancing to her food.

"Just text me when you're home later. I'll be working all day, but if you need anything, call me." Jamie smiles.

"Okay. I've got this if you need to head back for a meeting." She glances at her watch.

"Yes. Actually, I do. Thank you." She puts away the sandwich ingredients before saying goodbye to Millie. "I'll see you tomorrow after school. Have fun with Mama."

"Okay Mommy." She kisses her mom's cheek, and Jamie excuses herself to her office.

"Want to go to the park? Or what are you thinking?" I ask Millie. It's much easier to let her decide than taking her somewhere and she's a grump.

"Yes! The park! I wanna practice my swinging. Mary-Ann says she can do it to the sky, but I said that's not possible, but she swears it is so I'm going to see for myself. And if it's not I'm going to prove it to her tomorrow," Millie says between bites.

"Got it. Park it is." I support whatever beef she has with another six-year-old as much as I would with anyone else. Although I'm sure by the end of the week, the two of them will be best friends.

"All done." Millie hops off her chair and heads toward her room down the hall.

I take the plate, dump the excess food in the garbage, and clean the plate. Jamie always hated it when there was a single dish in the sink. It's something I'll never quite understand, but still, I don't want to leave it behind for her to do. Millie meets me by the front door with her weekend backpack and her school backpack. I have most of what she needs at my house, but there are a few things she likes to bring back and forth. It's usually her stuffy of the week and her sticker book.

I close the door behind us, knowing I don't have a key. Jamie has a Ring camera, so it isn't like anyone is breaking in—at least not without being caught. Millie and I toss her stuff in the trunk and then head for the park. There's one just outside of her school, and it's open on the days her school is closed. We stop at the bakery in town, Love in a Cup, and I grab an iced latte and get Millie a caffeine-free refresher. It's mainly juice, but I know she feels like a big kid drinking it.

"I'll be over here, okay?" I tell Millie as I grab a seat on the bench. It's in perfect view of the whole playground so I can see no matter where she runs.

"Okay!" She takes off in a run toward the swings.

"Is she your only?" a woman on the bench next to me asks.

"Oh, yeah. How about you?"

"I've got three of my own. Two are over there, and one's over there." She points to the different sides of the playground. "I'm Janet."

"Harmony." I shake her extended hand.

"I haven't seen you or your daughter around before, did you just move to town?" she asks, smiling. My defenses go up, but then immediately fall down. While in Chicago, if someone was asking so many questions about you, there was something up. This is a small town. The locals just want to get to know anyone new.

"We did. My ex-wife got a job here, so we moved at the end of the summer," I explain.

"Oh! You're Jamie's ex-wife? I met her at parent pickup. I thought your daughter looked familiar. It's Millie, right?"

"Yes." I nod.

"My daughter is Mary-Ann. I don't know if she's mentioned her."

I stifle a laugh; of course this is Mary-Ann's mother. "I don't think she has yet."

"They're in the same class. If they ever want to get together for a play date, I'd love to set something up," she says excitedly.

"Of course." I usually like to let Millie pick her own friends. I'll have to see how the swing fiasco goes before I commit her to any play dates.

"Mama! Look! Mary-Ann taught me how to jump rope!" Sure enough, Millie and Mary-Ann come running over with a purple jump rope to show me how she learned. If only adults could get along as easily as six-year-old children do.

"I love it!" I call out.

"Wanna exchange info?" Janet hands me her phone, and I add my number.

"Jamie and I split the week, so you might want to grab her number next time you see her."

"Gotcha, that's a good idea."

Millie and Mary-Ann keep jumping rope, and Janet goes back to reading her book. I attempt to relax, fidgeting a bit with the chip in my pocket. But one thing keeps popping back into my mind. I know I shouldn't be thinking about it, but every time I have a second, it comes back to the front of my mind. When I was working yesterday, between the saw being on and off, I heard Alana in the shower. Only, I don't think she was only showering. There was a plethora of moans and gasps as I heard the water going. I tried not to listen, but how can you not when it's coming out of the bathroom window right near where you're working? I have no clue if she did it on purpose or not. But I can still hear her breathy voice and the sounds she makes as she climaxes.

SEVEN

Alana

Maeve brought me everything I asked for and more—and the same night. She brought all my clothes, which I didn't ask about, and a variety of food. I was so grateful to have an apple and not a granola bar, I almost ate the whole bag of them. She didn't stay long and said she'd be back. She wasn't sure who had my phone, and it was complicated to ask for it without alerting more people. I forgot to tell her that Gemma had it. That thought occurred to me later on, but it's not like I'm desperate to make any calls.

Harmony didn't come yesterday. She left her schedule on a Post-it note on the fridge for me so I'd know when to expect her. She has a key, but she doesn't use it now that I'm here. I used her schedule to figure out when I should go for runs. I didn't want there to be any complications with the door being locked or unlocked without the other knowing.

Someone knocks on the front door, and I furrow my brow. Harmony isn't meant to be here for another hour, but maybe she's early? I open the front door without asking who it is, and I'm met with Norah's worried expression.

"You're hiding out somewhere, and you don't even ask who

it is?! You're just asking to be kidnapped!" she scolds me as she lets herself in.

"Norah? What are you doing here?" She hands me a bag of stuff and then plops on the couch, rubbing her pregnant stomach.

"It's too freaking hot out. I'm not even huge yet, but I swear this kid is like having a toaster attached to me all day long." Norah fans herself and touches her small but round belly.

"How did you know I'm here?" I raise an eyebrow.

"I didn't." She pauses. "I had a sneaking suspicion, but I didn't know for sure until you answered the door."

"Why did you *think* I'm here?" I clarify.

"Maeve was collecting your things and making a drop. She wouldn't explain where you were but said you were safe. But when you FaceTimed with Gemma and me, I recognized the wallpaper. It's the same in our kitchen. Which meant you had to be at one of the estate houses," Norah explains.

"Does anyone else know?"

"No. I'm going to tell Gemma when I get home. I can't keep secrets from her. But she doesn't need to come visit or anything. I just needed to see for myself that you're okay." Norah frowns.

"I am."

"You're not. But you're working on it."

"Is everyone mad at me?" I ask. "Wait, actually don't answer that. I don't think I want to know yet."

"Maeve said she brought you food and clothes. So I brought your record player. I remember how much you liked playing records whenever you were going through a breakup. I brought a few of your favorite albums, too." Norah smiles.

"Really?" I gasp.

"Yeah. It's in the car because it was too heavy for me to carry." She hesitates before adding, "You look a lot better than you did the day of the wedding. Calmer, more yourself."

"I feel calmer and more myself again."

"We all support you. We just want you to be happy. I don't

think you were with Will—not anymore anyway. So I'm glad you made the right call for you."

"I'm not trying to...I'm not meaning to hide out. I just need some time before I face everyone again." I sigh.

"I get it. I know it's different, but I took a lot of time after Finn died. So take all the time you need, just don't forget to come back to us when you're ready." Norah squeezes my hand.

A knock sounds on the door. "Alana? I'm here."

Harmony walks in with a T-shirt that says, *In loving memory of when I gave a fuck* and her tool belt tied to her tight jeans.

"Come in!" I call out as Norah eyeballs me.

"Oh, hello. I didn't realize...if you need me to come back later, I can," Harmony stutters as she sees Norah.

"No need. Norah this is Harmony. She's working on the renovations here. Harmony, this is my best friend, Norah. She's staying at one of the other houses on the property." Norah waves and Harmony smiles before excusing herself to work.

"Holy shit! You didn't tell me you're all cooped up with a hottie! No wonder you're feeling better!" Norah whispers.

"What? Harmony? Nah. She's just working on the kitchen and bathroom." I wave her off.

"She's hot. Like, the kind of hot that would be perfect for a rebound. You should definitely go for it." Norah winks.

"Not going to happen." I shake my head at her. She knows I've never been interested in women before, but then again, neither was she until Gemma.

"Are you ready to talk yet about the wedding?"

"No. I'm really not."

"Okay. When you are, just know we're here." Norah pats my hand. "Come get your record player out of the car, and I'll leave you alone."

I follow her outside and grab it from her trunk. It's in an oversized box so it won't get ruined, even though it's in its case. Norah and I say goodbye, and she heads home. I bring the record player into the living room and look through the records she brought me. Fleetwood Mac, Olivia Rodrigo, Lana Del Rey, and Pink. I'm not in the mood to listen to them, but I'm happy to have them.

When I went through bad breakups in high school and college, I didn't leave my room for days. I just blared music and snacked on fried food my sister snuck me. I was probably depressed, but my mother is one of those people who thinks you can cure depression by going outside more. Music has always been there for me, and it got me through the rough times.

I dig through the bag Norah brought me and realize it contains my phone and charger, along with a journal, some fancy pens, my current glasses, and some contacts—which I'm sure Norah added herself. I've never been one to journal, but maybe I'll try it and see if it helps. It isn't like it can do more harm at this point.

I retreat to the bedroom with my supplies, spreading them out on the bed. I rip open the package of pens, take the plastic off the journal, and sigh. I took a creative writing course in college. I know how to write a story, but I don't know how to write what I'm feeling. It isn't like anyone will ever see this. Maybe it'll help get me out of this funk.

~~Dear Diary~~

I strike that out because I feel twelve, and this is supposed to be therapeutic.

I don't exactly know what I'm supposed to write in this. I've never been someone who documents her feelings. Probably because it's often easier for me to push them aside. With my mother and Wrenn, I was always the middle-man, trying to keep the peace between them from a young age. So it only makes sense that I kept doing the same thing as I got older.

The things I wanted didn't seem to matter to Will anymore. He was always siding with my mother or his mother or anyone other than me. It was easier to pretend that was okay than to fight him on it and watch him retreat. I was tired of fighting. I just wanted someone to ask me what I wanted and for once, go with it.

I think leaving the wedding was the first time I recognized myself. I was standing in a gown I didn't love, flowers that weren't my favorite, and everything that looked picture perfect. Except deep down, I knew I couldn't go on like that. I wish I had enough guts to tell Will myself. It pains me knowing he had to hear it from someone else. But I also know I wouldn't have been strong enough to leave had I told him myself. Somehow, he would've convinced me to stay. He would've said that it was cold feet like I always said, and he would've told me to just get down the aisle.

But I didn't want that. I didn't want my parents' marriage, or his parents'. I just wanted someone who wanted the same things I wanted. Not in the big things like he felt, but in how I hate the crusts of sandwiches, and I love PDA. I wanted to feel loved more than tolerated. That my likes weren't childish or crazy. I wanted to feel like I could be myself in a marriage. Living the rest of my life in hiding wasn't something I wanted to do.

A lone tear falls on the page, and I realize I'm crying. I didn't realize how much I was holding back until I wrote it down. How long had I been feeling this way? Making everyone else's lives easy and convenient while mine was becoming hell. I couldn't recall the last time I had let myself be happy at someone else's expense. I never want to cause anyone harm, but why am I so okay with putting that harm on me? I pick up the pen and start writing again.

I'm still not ready to talk to anyone about this. I feel like it would be too much to unload on anyone. Everyone has their own stuff going on. I can't drag them into this. Maybe that was why I let myself get all the way to the aisle with a man I wasn't 100% sure of.

Whenever I think about Will, I get a mixture of angry and

sad. He changed more than I thought he would since the time I met him. The pressure of his parents' company on his back, shutting me out instead of leaning on me, and the way he claimed to love me but was so different when we were alone. Too many nights we both slept apart, me sleeping in the guest room or him sleeping on the couch. For a lot of the last month, we had avoided each other. Every time I tried connecting with him, like at the carnival, we would fight. All I had done was try to kiss him with some powdered sugar on my lips and he freaked out. Not wanting PDA, FROM HIS FIANCÉE. Not wanting to kiss me with something on my lips and then berating me for getting sugar on his shirt. I spent the night crying at Norah and Gemma's, and the next day, he didn't say a word about it. Is that how I'm supposed to live the rest of my life? Pretending things are great when they aren't?

I saw the way my friends interacted with their girlfriends. Each relationship is different, but none of them act the way Will acted with me. I want someone who would claim me in public as much as they would in private. Someone who won't care if there's food on my face and laugh with me. I want someone I can let down my inhibitions with and know it won't lead to a fight. I also want someone who will stand up for me, whether it be against my mother or his mother or someone else.

I close the book and toss it on the nightstand. I let out as much as I can for now. It hurts too much to go any deeper. No one expects things to be fixed overnight. Maybe I can do it one page at a time. I slide under the covers and force my eyes shut. I know I'm not going to sleep anytime soon, but I need to lie here and shut out the world for a little bit.

EIGHT

Harmony

When I pull up to the house, it's later than normal. I had a million things to do at home today, and I knew Alana wouldn't mind if I came late. I knock on the front door but there's music blasting from inside. I press my ear to the door to see if I can place the song. It sounds like something I've heard before but I'm not sure what it is. I knock a little louder and wait, but when it's clear Alana can't hear me, I unlock the door. I quietly enter and see Alana dancing in the living room. She's wearing a blanket as a cape and using a spatula as a makeshift microphone. Alana belts out the lyrics to a song I definitely don't know while she shakes her body around. She's not facing me, so she still hasn't noticed I'm here yet.

I quietly put down my tools and stand still, waiting for a moment to say something. I also can't help but admire her. Alana's dark curls cascade down the back of the blanket, and I can see her half smile as she dances around the room. She looks more relaxed than I've ever seen her. I guess this is what she does to relax. It's nice to see her so happy for once. Part of me wonders if I should leave and give her this space.

"Holy shit!" Alana gasps and drops the spatula onto the couch. "You scared the crap out of me!"

"I'm sorry. I knocked." I wince.

"I shouldn't have had the music so loud." She blushes a bright pink. Her high cheekbones lighting up with color.

"It's totally fine, it was nice to see you happy," I admit.

"Thanks." She pauses the record and bites her bottom lip. Then she picks up a glass of red wine and takes a long sip. Ah, so she's been drinking. Maybe that's why she's a bit more relaxed.

"Do you want some? I have more in the kitchen," she asks, catching my gaze on the glass.

"No thanks." I shake my head.

"Okay, well if you change your mind."

I clench my fist, wishing I could. Wishing I could taste it on her lips. The sweet taste of Alana's lips and the alcohol I crave. I put my hand in my pocket, grab ahold of my five year chip, and ground myself. I didn't need a drink.

"I'll be in the back." I excuse myself to start working.

Alana is a vixen, inherently sexy despite her not trying to be. She is so freaking gorgeous without any effort. I know it's silly; she's probably straight and doesn't notice me. But here I am crushing on the straight woman. I try to focus on grouting the tile like I'm supposed to be, but as the music starts playing again, I'm a little distracted. I can imagine her hips swaying, her pink lips on the side of the wine glass, and her voice belting out lyrics. She has a pretty good voice, all things considered.

Shaking my head, I look back at the wood I've cut and decide to get to work on making the new shelf storage for over the toilet. All the wood was already cut so I basically just needed to put it together. A few nails and an anchor—I should be done with it in two hours tops. I push all thoughts of Alana from my mind and get to work. I can do this; I've worked with horny housewives before. But working with a woman who I'm so clearly crushing on is crazy.

At least an hour passes before I take a break for some water. My water bottle needs refilling, so I head to the kitchen to get some fresh tap water. There's one of those filter things on the faucet, so it's okay to drink. Alana's still dancing in the living room, this time without any blanket. I notice she's changed the album to a Fleetwood Mac one. *Rumors*, I think it is. She's swaying her hips as I take a long sip from my water bottle.

"Hey! Watching me again?" Alana catches me this time, and I cough, choking on the water.

Her eyes widen as she realizes her mistake and comes running over. "I'm okay," I choke out.

"Please don't choke, I doubt my parents' insurance covers that," she jokes.

"I wasn't watching, just getting some water," I mumble.

"Oh, I know." She laughs.

"You have good taste in music. This is a really good album." I smile.

"Thanks, it's one of my favorites. My fiancé used to hate when I played it. He only had a thing for music without any lyrics." She makes a face, scrunching her nose.

"Oh no. That's the worst, how do you sing along to something with no words?" I shake my head.

"It was one of the things we disagreed on." She sighs and sinks into the couch.

"Were you with him long?" I don't know much about him, or the wedding, or her. So I tread lightly with my questions.

"We were together since college. So like, five years, just about."

"And were you engaged long?"

"A year. He wanted to live together first, which made sense. His family and my family come from money, so he wanted to make sure we were doing this for the right reasons." She shrugs. I can tell she's feeling much more open because of the wine.

"I was married. My ex-wife, she's great now. But we fought like hell for years and disagreed on mostly everything." I figure I should share something.

"Will and I weren't like that at first, we didn't really fight.

He'd disagree with me and then disappear into our room until he could pretend it didn't happen. It got worse with the wedding because I couldn't do everything on my own, and he liked giving into his parents since they were paying for the wedding."

"Do you think that's worse?"

"What?" She tilts her head sideways.

"Him ignoring the issues and pretending they didn't happen. Do you think that's worse than just fighting about it?"

"I never really thought about it. I didn't realize how much I was ignoring things myself until one of my friends pointed it out. Of course, I yelled at her for that. But now I see she was right all along. I was blinded by love, I guess." Alana takes a sip of wine.

"Do you feel better now?"

"I do. I'm relieved I'm not married. I wish I had realized it sooner and saved everyone's time and money though."

"I think that's a good thing. You shouldn't feel bad about realizing your worth and not jumping into something you realize you no longer wanted."

"It's just hard. I haven't been able to see or really talk to anyone. My friends brought me things, but I'm terrified to even turn on my phone. I don't know how I'm going to face everyone, especially Will."

"Was Will your fiancé?"

"Yeah."

"Has he reached out?"

"Yeah, I saw some messages, but I didn't read them. I'm not ready to."

"Will you ever be ready to?"

"What do you mean?"

"I just don't think anyone's ever *ready* to do something they know will cause pain. But it might be better in the long run if you get it over with. You might be pushing off the inevitable." I shrug.

"I, uh, didn't really think of it like that. I just figured it might be easier to talk to him once the sting has worn off. But I guess you're right, that might not happen." She studies me for a moment. "You still talk to your ex-wife?"

That catches me off guard. "What?"

"Well, you said she's good now. I don't know many divorced people who still speak to their ex-wives." Her dark eyebrows scrunch together in confusion.

"We have a child together. My daughter, Millie, who's six. I kind of don't have a choice but to communicate with her," I explain.

"Oh, that makes sense." She nods. "I'm sorry for, like, unloading all this on you. You're basically a stranger, and I'm a mess talking about my ex-fiancé and all my issues."

"I don't mind."

"Really?"

"If you need someone to talk to, I'm here. I don't mind getting to know you." It's the truth.

The more I learn about Alana, the more I'm captivated by her. She isn't some princess who ran out on her wedding to screw everyone over. She's someone who finally listened to her heart instead of everyone around her and hurt a lot of people. But she's tortured by how much pain she brought because of being happy. It's probably also kept her from being happy in the past. She's a bit too much of a people pleaser, it seems. It only makes me want to help her find her voice.

"You might regret that." She laughs. "Do you have a picture of your daughter?"

"I do." I pull out my phone and lean over to show the most recent one of her on the first day of school. A big, toothy smile and her unicorn dress.

"She's gorgeous. She has your eyes." Alana looks up at mine and back at the photo a few times.

"Thanks, it's actually probably the donor we chose. My ex-wife carried her," I explain.

"Hmm, that's interesting."

I'm sitting on the edge of one couch, holding my phone toward her while she's leaning over the arm of the other couch. She's holding the empty glass of wine, but I smell it on her breath. It's bitter, and yet I know the taste would be sweet. I inhale, being reminded of my old friend and tempted by the woman with the most kissable lips. But as she leans forward just a tad, I pull back and stand up abruptly.

"I should get back to work," I announce and avoid eye contact with her.

"Of course. I should get ready for bed." Her voice is shaky.

I go to the bathroom and lock the door behind me. I need a moment to breathe. I reach in my pocket and wrap my fingers around the chip again. I am here, I didn't take a drink, and I'm still sober. Alana probably thinks I rejected her, and in some ways, I did. I'd never kiss a clearly drunk woman. But I jumped up because I was more tempted by the wine than I was Alana. The thought of kissing her is nothing compared to getting to taste wine again. Her lips and breath were covered in it, and I couldn't let that go. I know I need time and distance from that if I'm going to make the right choice.

I hate this. I hate that I'm five years sober, and the fucking smell of wine is still tempting to me. Is it because it's on her lips? I can't remember the last time I was around someone who drank. I don't like it around me, because why tempt fate? And drunk people when you're sober? A fucking nightmare.

I know I like Alana. It isn't like I'm only attracted to the alcohol, but I can't be near her, let alone kiss her, with wine on her lips. It's a gateway to buying myself a pint of whiskey and blacking out. I can't do that. The image of Millie pops into my head. I head out of the bathroom and unlock the back door to hit my vape. I need a few hits, and I can't risk running into Alana right now. I decide to dial Ruby while I'm at it. I don't know what time it is in Chicago, but she always picks up for me.

NINE

Alana

After talking with Harmony about everything that went down, I do feel a little bit better. I know I spilled too much to a total stranger, but I felt like I *could*. Maybe it was the wine I'd had two glasses of, or just finally talking about it felt good. But either way, I liked how safe I felt talking with Harmony. She didn't judge, thinking carefully before asking me something. I didn't have to put on any kind of facade or try to make her happy. We existed—coexisted.

And then I had to ruin it all by leaning in to kiss her. I must've read the vibe wrong and became a lightweight since I hadn't been drinking much lately. I should've known better than to kiss someone. And a woman at that. I'm not even into women. Sure they're hot, and I'd noticed more than a few in my life. But I've never *liked* a woman like that. Maybe I'm just lonely. Which is probably why I was so relieved when Maeve showed up at my door today.

"Thank you again. You really don't have to keep coming by with food," I tell Maeve after she's dropped off groceries for the second week in a row.

"I know, but I really don't mind," she insists.

"Do you want to sit and hang out a bit? I'm starting to miss seeing people," I admit. Maybe even a little more since Harmony dodged my drunken kiss.

"Of course." Maeve sits on the couch across from me and waits for me to say something.

"I appreciate you not telling anyone where I was. Norah found me anyway and came to see me. She brought me my phone, but I haven't had the courage to open it yet."

"I'm sure you will when you feel up to it. I recently received a box of things that survived my apartment building fire. I don't think I'll ever feel ready to open that," she says shakily. Heather had mentioned how her brother died in that fire, so I don't blame her. It was bad enough losing her home, I couldn't imagine losing a family member too.

"I just don't know what to say to everyone. I miss my friends and my family. But I don't know how to talk to them after this," I admit.

"I mean, I've never run away from a wedding before. So I don't know how you're feeling, but maybe start off small. With whoever you think would take it the best. Your ex-fiancé might need some building up to. But your friends just miss you."

"You're right." I nod.

"I'm happy you finally feel like opening up."

"I talked a bit with the handywoman, Harmony. I think it's easier to talk to people who don't know me as well, and who weren't at the wedding."

"Was she a good listener?"

"She was. She let me vent about my issues until…"

"Until?" Maeve raises an eyebrow.

"I stupidly made a pass at her. I was a little wine drunk and leaned in to kiss her." I sigh.

"Oh, are you attracted to women?"

"No, I mean, not really. Everyone has fantasies about women, right?"

"Uh, not really, actually. I have some very straight friends who are quite disgusted by the sight of boobs," Maeve says with a light laugh. She isn't judging, but I can tell she's treading lightly.

"But I mean, I've only ever dated men. I've only ever liked men. I can't suddenly be a lesbian, right?"

"Well, no, but I think it's more like a scale. Some people favor more attraction in one way or the other. And then there's always being Pansexual, where you're more attracted to the *who* and not what parts they may have."

I contemplate her words. Norah and Gemma were a surprise for me. Norah had only been with men, she'd married a man, and then she fell in love with Gemma. *Am I like that?*

"I'd also add that you just went through a *huge* life change. You might be looking for connection, especially while in isolation. I wouldn't try to label yourself unless that's something you need. But instead, think about the motivations behind it," Maeve continues.

"That makes sense. I'm the last person in the world who should be looking to date or even kiss anyone." I laugh.

All of a sudden, I hear the key in the front door, and I look at it, confused. Harmony isn't coming to work today, but maybe she forgot something. Sometimes she comes by just to measure something.

"Alana Margaret Thomas. Do you want to tell me what the hell you're doing here?" my mother yells. My eyes go wide as I see her walking into the house with her phone in hand, showing me grabbing the hidden key the night I ran away from the wedding.

"Mom?" My dad trails in behind her with a sullen look on his face.

"Your father and I were checking up on the handyman. I wanted to be sure she was coming and going as she said, so imagine my surprise when I find out that's where my daughter —who ran away from her wedding—was hiding."

"I'm going to go, but let me know if you need anything," Maeve begins to excuse herself.

"Oh sure, now that you've helped aiding and abetting my daughter." My mother scoffs.

"Mom, I'm not a criminal."

"You might as well be. You ran away on your wedding day and it took days to find you. Do you know how much stress that's been for us?" My mother is a bit dramatic, but I knew they'd be upset.

"I'm sorry."

"You're sorry!? Do you know how embarrassing it was for us to stand in front of Will's parents and say we didn't know where you were?! That you went for a walk and never came back?!" she screams.

"I'm sorry it was embarrassing for you that I didn't want to get married." I clench my fist.

"Alana dear, there were more opportune times for you to say something if you didn't want to be married," my dad says quietly.

"ANYTIME would be better than on your wedding day, FIFTEEN MINUTES before you're due to go down the aisle," my mother adds.

"I knew you'd be upset..."

My mother cuts me off. "Of course we're upset! We're all ready to get you married and you go missing! It was like we were on one of your father's shows!" My dad was a big fan of any detective show, especially *Law and Order: SVU*.

"I'm sorry I didn't tell anyone where I was going. It's not like I planned it." I sigh.

"Do you know how embarrassing it is to have to call the police?! Will was devastated."

"I know."

"You know? And you're okay hiding out here with one of your friends when the man you were going to marry is miserable and confused?!" My mother throws her hands in the air.

"We're glad you're okay, sweetheart, but we're just confused. I thought everything was good. You seemed so happy when you got engaged." My father sits on the couch next to me and looks to me for some answers.

"I was." I start to cry.

"So what changed?" he asks softly.

"He did. He's not the same man I fell in love with. And despite everything being perfect and everyone wanting me to be with him, I just couldn't do it. I didn't want to pretend anymore."

"So there's no chance you're going back to him?" my mother asks.

I quickly turn to face her. "What?"

"I mean there's nothing he could do or say to get you back?"

"No. I don't think he'd even want to get back together, all things considered." I scoff.

"He does. He told me he just wants you."

"You talked to him?" I look at my dad, but he looks just as shocked by this as I do.

"He called, asking if I'd seen you. I told him the truth, and he said he just wants to know what went wrong. He said he just wants to see you again."

"Okay, but that doesn't mean..."

My mother cuts me off again. "Just because you've been a little unhappy isn't a good reason to turn away a good man. You're almost thirty, and it's not like you have other options."

My jaw drops. Is my mother serious? Surely, she isn't saying this to my face. I must be hearing her incorrectly. She's said some out-of-pocket things to Wrenn over the years, but this? I just turned twenty-eight and it's not like I'm some ugly and horrific person. I could find someone else if I wanted. For some reason, Harmony pops into my head, but I don't say anything.

"I'm not getting back together with him. I don't love him," I say firmly.

"Will you at least consider coming home? You can stay with us until you get back on your feet. It's not good to be here while someone's doing work. You shouldn't be breathing any chemicals." My dad frowns.

"Harmony doesn't use anything harmful in the house. She's working outside if there's anything strong, and she always warns me."

"So you've seen her? You're what, hanging out with the handyman?" My mother rolls her eyes.

"We've talked a few times. She's usually working so I try not to bother her." It isn't a lie.

"I just feel like I don't know you anymore. You run out on your wedding, you don't come home. Where did we go wrong?" My mother lets out a dramatic sigh.

"You didn't *go wrong*. Shouldn't you be happy that your daughter didn't submit herself to a lifelong marriage she wasn't happy in?"

"Not everything is perfect all the time, Alana," she says.

"No. It's not. But I deserve someone who wants us to be as close as we can to that. Someone who actually loves me and not just the idea of me. I know I need to talk to Will, and I promise to reach out. But I'm not sorry for finally putting myself first. I did what I felt was right. What I thought I needed, and I have never felt so relieved. If I were coming home from my honeymoon today, married to Will, I'd be miserable." I stand, making sure I don't lose my nerve. My mother opens her mouth, but I think I've rendered her speechless because she closes it just as quick.

"Please promise you'll think about coming home soon. Or at least not hiding out here," my dad insists.

"I promise I'm not going to live here. I just need more time before I come back to the world."

"Okay." My dad gives me a hug, pulling me in tight.

"I'm not going to be a willing participant in whatever crisis this is. You're too young to be having a midlife crisis, so knock it off and come home soon." My mother leaves without a look back.

My dad sighs and follows after her. We both know it will be

worse for him later if he doesn't. I lock the door behind them and slump against it, my knees sliding to the ground. I feel like I just ran a marathon in that conversation. My hands were shaking the whole time I was speaking back to my mother, but I don't think she noticed.

There's no doubt in my mind that my mother will tell Will where I am. It's only a matter of time. So I gather all my strength to find my phone and read the messages from him I missed. I'll debate giving him a phone call and maybe telling him where I am first. I know I owe him an explanation, I just hope it will go better than it did with my parents.

TEN

Harmony

I'm sitting in the back of a random AA meeting because I can't get Alana out of my head. Ruby talked me off a cliff last week, and I've been careful ever since. She said I made the right move, for so many reasons. But now I feel like whatever wall that was coming down between Alana and me has just gone back up. I don't know what to do, so I sit in a random meeting hoping something someone says will make sense to me.

I drink the terrible coffee and wonder if this is a staple of every AA meeting. Like we aren't allowed to have good coffee because it's just another addiction. Either way, I'm focusing on the speaker talking about their lowest moment, and all I can think about is Alana. The body she has, her lips, and how I love just talking to her. She opened up so much to me, and it felt like she was finally relaxing—until I had to run away and make her put her guard back up.

Sure, I know it wasn't literally my fault. But I don't know how to tell her I want to kiss her, and it was actually the alcohol I was running from and not her. There's nothing casual about that.

"Anyone else want to speak?" the meeting leader asks.

I raise my hand, and he waves me up.

"Hi, I'm Harmony, and I'm an alcoholic."

An array of *hellos* greet me.

"I'm currently five years and seventeen days sober. I recently had the opportunity to kiss someone I sort of like, but they had just drank some wine. I was going for it until I had to run away. I knew if I kissed her in that moment, I'd only be thinking about the wine. I live my life soberly, and I haven't been around alcohol in years. Am I going to have to find someone who's also sober? Is that my only option? I thought after the years it might get easier, but feeling how I felt, I know it only takes a second to throw it all away. Now I might have messed up things with this woman, and I'm not even sure where to go from here. I feel like she's avoiding me, and I don't know if I'm supposed to tell her the truth so early on and hope she gets it, or just find someone who doesn't drink at all so there are no temptations. That's my share, thank you."

I feel better getting that off my chest. Sometimes I wish people were allowed to respond to shares because it would be more helpful for someone to tell me what I needed to be doing. But then again, it was probably better that I figure everything out for myself. It was like I was a teenager all over again and my mother was telling me I needed to learn the lesson the hard way. She usually wasn't right, but in this particular case, I knew she was.

Someone else goes up to share and I take my seat again. I sip the end of my coffee and place the cup on the floor next to me. Maybe it's better this way. I've only had a handful of relationships since I got sober. Most people are okay with me not drinking, but as soon as I can't be around them drinking, things get complicated. Add on the fact that I'm divorced and have a child —most of my relationships are casual. You don't often see too many women signing up to date someone with so much baggage.

I'm probably getting ahead of myself with Alana anyway. It isn't like we've talked that many times, who knows what she's even thinking. I should probably get to know her better before I tried to start anything there.

The meeting ends, and after we clean up, I head out. I don't have to work on the project today, but I drive in the direction of the house anyway. I don't realize what I'm doing there until I knock on the door and see Alana.

"Harmony! What's up? Did I forget you're working tonight?" She looks confused as she opens the door. She's dressed in a fluffy robe over a pink pajama set of a cami top and shorts. Fuck, and she definitely isn't wearing a bra.

Focusing back on her face, I clear my throat. "I wanted to talk to you, can I come in?"

"Sure." Alana nods and I close the door behind us. "I was just about to pour myself a glass of wine do you want one?"

"No thanks."

"So what's going on? Did my parents confront you about being here or something?" She glances past me as if they're about to barge in.

"No, no, this is about me."

"Oh, okay." She pulls out the bottle of wine from the fridge and pops the cork.

I take a breath as she grabs a glass from the cabinet.

"You sure you don't want anything to drink?" Alana asks again. She's pouring herself a glass of red wine.

I close my eyes with my back to her and say, "I'm an alcoholic."

Pin drop silence fills the air. Alana stops pouring and I open my eyes before turning around. Then she's pouring her glass of wine down the drain and about to do the same with the bottle.

"What are you doing?" I ask, confused.

"I had no idea. I'm glad you told me. I'll get rid of this."

"You can still drink. I'm the one who can't drink."

"It's not like it's something I need. If this is what you came to talk about, you clearly have a hard time being around it, and I'm sorry. I wish I knew." She frowns.

"I-I'm usually fine..."

"But? It seems like that was an unfinished thought."

"It's part of why I didn't kiss you that night. Why I wanted to kiss you but couldn't. Because I knew if I did, I'd only want to drink."

"You wanted to kiss me?" Her eyes meet mine. *Shit.* I didn't mean to say that part.

"I've been sober for five years. I try not to be around alcohol, so I'm not asking you to stop drinking. I'm just asking you to stop asking me to drink with you. Because I'm afraid one day I might say yes."

"Because you want to kiss me?" Her eyes widen.

"Well, partially yes," I admit. "I'm attracted to you, and when you tried to kiss me, all I could smell was the wine on your breath. So I ran, not because of you but because I can't be tempted by alcohol like that."

"So you didn't run from me because I tried to kiss you?" she asks quietly.

"No, and if I knew how to tell you that without sounding crazy, I would've told you weeks ago." I laugh.

"I thought you just weren't attracted to me."

"I'm so attracted to you it's insane," I admit.

"I-I—" She starts to stutter but I cut her off.

"You don't have to say anything. I was just coming over to ask if you could keep the drinking to a minimum around me and definitely not ask me if I want any."

"I completely understand. I'm glad you told me." A soft smile plays on her lips.

"Well, I'll see you tomorrow then." I turn to go but she calls after me.

"I'm attracted to you, too," Alana says, grabbing my arm. "I wasn't going to say anything, and I probably shouldn't be saying anything because this is crazy. But I am attracted to you, but I don't think I'm supposed to date or even be with anyone right now. My life's a mess, and I'm a mess..."

I cut her off by placing two fingers on her lips. Her eyes flutter to meet mine, and I smile. Her dark brown eyes feel like warmth and ease. God, she is so fucking beautiful. I think about kissing her. About telling her I don't care about how much of a mess she is because I'm a mess too. We could be messes together. I think she wants to kiss me too because she holds eye contact with me, and it's like I can feel the tension building between us. The invisible tension that feels like flames growing between us. I can feel it like a string pulling me toward her, the tension against my body as I move back. I move my fingers from her lips and look at her mouth.

She's switching between looking at my mouth and looking into my eyes. Neither of us move; I think we're afraid to ruin the moment or break the eye contact. It's like a sexual staring contest and the prize is getting the other. Her pretty pink lips pucker just slightly, and if you weren't looking you'd miss it. Her face softens, and she almost leans my way. And that's when I know.

"I'm not going to kiss you," I tell her quietly. She looks surprised. I think I've even surprised myself.

"I want more than to just be attracted to you. I want you to be sure of what you want before I kiss you. I don't want to be just another person to you. There's no rush," I say.

"Okay." She nods.

"I'll see you tomorrow."

Alana closes the front door behind me, and I don't breathe normally until I'm back at the car. I can feel Alana's lips on my fingers. I brush them over my own lips, knowing that's the closest I'll be getting to her lips for a while. She is so cute when she starts rambling on and on. I knew she was going to talk herself to death. She isn't ready for anything, but I can wait. I'm patient, and the last thing either of us need is to rush into anything. She was engaged a few weeks ago, I don't expect her to suddenly be ready for something with someone new.

Jamie and I had rushed into things. We were nineteen, thinking our love would last forever. Looking back on it now, I know we were just kids in that puppy love stage of things. We got married after only months of knowing each other, thinking the honeymoon phase would last forever. Being newlyweds was fun until reality kicked in. But then we focused so hard on big things that were supposed to keep us happy. We bought a house, we tried having a baby, we got careers. But despite it all, we were never as happy as I thought we'd be. We fought like hell, and it only got worse when my drinking started. We'd be up until two in the morning fighting and having sex and then fighting again. Always screaming at each other and never actually resolving anything.

Part of me has always wondered if Jamie and I had taken more time in the beginning, really gotten to know each other, what would've happened. Would we have still gotten married? Fizzled out completely in the beginning? If I hadn't started drinking, would we still be together? If I got sober faster, would I still be married? I try to think it doesn't matter. We got Millie, and that's the one good thing both of us can agree on. She was never a regret or a mistake. We just wish it had been easier for us to stay a family.

So I know I want to take things slow with Alana. Really get to know her before anything happens. I want to bring her life ease and joy, not more mess and stress. I just want to be there to hear about her day and talk to her the way we have been. So as much as I want to kiss her, I know I need to keep myself in check. It'll be better that way.

ELEVEN

Alana

"Move your ass if you want to keep it! I'm trying to hug my sister!" Wrenn yells, hip checking Ryleigh out of the way so she can hug me.

"Babe, you'll pay for that later." Ryleigh laughs.

"I can't believe I actually missed you." Wrenn squeezes me tightly and then ruffles my hair for good measure.

"I missed you too, little sis." I smile.

Everyone takes their turns hugging me and holding me tightly. I invited everyone over for a slumber party just like we used to do back in high school. Now, of course, with Gemma and Maeve and Sage added to the group. I also invited Kim's girlfriend, Zara, but she's on tour with her new book so she sent us a platter of cookies in her place.

I pull Kim to the hallway when she walks in. I want a chance to apologize to her myself. "I'm so sorry about everything that went down before the wedding. I know you were just looking out for me. I should've believed you, but I was trying so hard to keep believing the facade. I'm really sorry and I hope you can forgive me."

"Of course I can. I never wanted you to cancel your wedding or anything, I just wanted to see you stand up for yourself. You deserve the world and someone who treats you as such. I couldn't imagine you marrying him without me at least warning you," Kim explains.

"I know. I see it now, I really do. He did so many terrible things and I tried to explain them off. But in reality, he's just a shitty guy."

"He really is." Kim laughs.

"Thank you all for coming. I'm so sorry I've been MIA. I promise to answer any questions anyone might have," I say as we all get settled in the living room.

I moved some of the couches back, the coffee table to my bedroom, and made enough space for everyone to have a spot. We'd scatter among the five bedrooms later and some on the couches. There should be enough room for everyone. It's not like any of us are scared of sharing with someone else.

"We're just all relieved you're okay. Please never hide from us again," Norah says with a nervous laugh.

"I promise." I smile. Her cheeks have gotten a little rounder, just like her belly. I'm not sure how many weeks she is now, but her cute little baby bump has popped. Even in her flannel pajamas, you can see a clear baby bump.

"How the hell did you get here from the hotel?" Gemma asks.

"I took a cab, then begged him to wait while I ran in here for cash. Thank God, my parents forgot about it." I shrug.

"I don't need any details, but are you living here now or is this temporary?" Heather asks.

"I think it's temporary. I'm still on leave from work until the end of the month, so I don't have to worry about that. But I do need to find a new place to live since Will kind of lives in our old place."

"Have you spoken to him?" Ryleigh asks.

"No. He sent me a few texts after the wedding, but I haven't had the guts to call him or anything."

Will had sent me exactly three texts on the day of our wedding and then silence since.

Will: Where are you?

Will: This isn't funny. Where the hell did you go? Your mother says she can't find you??

Will: I will never forgive you for this.

The last one seemed more angry than the others. But at least he isn't still freaking out and texting me. Or showing up here now that my mother probably told him I was here.

"Serves his ass right." Wrenn grunts and Ryleigh shoves her.

"I feel so bad I made everyone get dresses and come to a wedding that didn't even happen. I just saw the decorations and everything and started to panic. But once I saw Wrenn and Ryleigh holding hands, I knew I couldn't go through with it," I explain.

"Us?" Wrenn looks at me confused.

"You and Ryleigh held hands, and it just clicked. Will never held my hand in public—or in private for that matter. I just wanted someone who *wanted* to hold my hand. It should be as simple as it seems, like what most of you have. Why would I want something I constantly have to work on for the rest of my life? That's not a marriage, that's a job."

"I'm so glad you figured that out before you were tied to him forever," Gemma says.

"I really appreciate you all giving me some space before I was ready to talk about this. I just needed some time, but now I'm so glad to have you all back here." I smile.

"Good, because we'll all be taking turns visiting you until you get sick of us." Ryleigh laughs.

"I mean, it's not like I've been here alone this whole time." I chew on my bottom lip.

"Are you blushing?!" Wrenn squeals.

"Tell us everything!" Kim smiles.

"There's a woman who's been here working on the house. My parents hired her, and I had no clue she'd be here, but she's also been pretty good at keeping my secret."

"A woman?" Heather raises an eyebrow.

I know what they're all thinking.

"I don't know. She's just so different. And I think I'm attracted to her. We almost kissed one night, and my body was on fire for hours after. And she didn't even touch me!" I exclaim.

"How did our group go from mostly straight to no straights?" Norah laughs.

"I'm not ready to label anything, but she's just so freaking hot," I say.

"What does she look like? Do you know her Instagram?" Sage asks.

"Oh, yeah! Let's look her up!" Heather exclaims happily.

"I do actually." I stand and grab her business card from the fridge and let them know her social media handle.

"It's loading!" Heather announces over Sage's shoulder.

Everyone huddles over her and they all gasp when the page loads.

"Holy shit," Ryleigh mumbles.

"She looks like an off-brand Halsey with the blue hair. Like when Halsey went through that era?" Heather says.

"She does!" Wrenn exclaims.

"I'm impressed; you should go for it." Gemma nods her approval.

"I don't know if there's anything to *go* for. But I like talking to her, and I wouldn't mind if she kissed me." I don't mention what she said to me last time we almost kissed. That feels like something I want to keep between us for now.

"I feel like I've stepped into the twilight zone." Wrenn laughs.

"Why?" I ask.

"Because you of all people is talking about *maybe* kissing a woman and you left Will at the altar. The most savage way to break up with someone. I'm just impressed. I didn't know this version of you existed." Wrenn shrugs.

"I think it's always been here; I was just more worried about keeping everyone else happy. I'm trying to find joy in my life that only matters to me right now," I explain.

"Well, we're all here for it." Wrenn smiles.

My friends break off into chatter about different things. We talk about how Kim is going to visit Zara in New York next week for a long weekend. Norah talks about how she's almost done renovating the apartment for her and the baby. Gemma gushes over how Norah chose the giraffe theme that she picked out. Heather is still looking for a place to live in town but hasn't had anything in her price range pop up. I assure her that she and Maeve can live there as long as they need. Gemma already talked to me about staying in the estate house until Norah is ready for her to move in. She didn't say it in that many words, but I know that's what she's waiting for on. Ryleigh and Wrenn talk about how they're going to spend the next few months traveling to different countries. They're starting in Paris and working their way around Europe for a bit. I have to admit I'm jealous and joke that I might have to visit them when they get to Italy.

We order some pizzas and talk about putting a movie on, but none of us actually agree on what we might want to watch. So instead, the TV stays off and we all talk the night away instead. I can't remember the last time I laughed and smiled as hard as this.

Norah's the first to fall asleep. She curls up on Gemma's lap, and she's out within minutes. Gemma slips a blanket over her and plays with her hair while she sleeps. We all keep hanging out, but I feel a jealous pang as I watch the way they are. It's so evident that Gemma loves Norah. I don't know how I didn't see it before. But the way they are together—they both look to each other, even when the other isn't paying attention. They know what the other needs without any words spoken between them. It's something I long for.

Will never knew what I needed, and if I said what I needed, it didn't mean he'd listen. I always felt we were two people living different lives. When it was just us, every so often I'd feel a spark again. But most of the time it was me hoping for a sign that it was the right thing to be with him. Every time I'd begin to question things, it was like he'd know and start trying harder again. But now I can see that with real love, the love my friends have, it's often effortless. They aren't overthinking and worrying about how to make the other happy. Just their presence makes the other calm, and everything else is a bonus.

"I'm so glad you decided to invite everyone over. And thank you for including me," Maeve whispers, taking an open spot next to me on the couch.

"Of course. It just felt like it was time. I needed my people. And you're one of them now." I smile at her.

"I am?"

"Hell yeah. You're one of us, and that means you're stuck with us. So you better be prepared for that," I tease.

Maeve just smiles and I know she's relieved to be a part of this. I'm sure she has other friends too, but it never hurts to have a few more. I reach for her hand and squeeze it softly.

"Wait!" Heather says. "Who's watching Cheeto if you're going to Europe?"

We all look at Ryleigh and Wrenn, who look at me.

"We were going to ask you to watch him." Wrenn smiles.

"What!? I want him." Heather frowns.

"You can take him." I laugh.

"Really?" Heather perks up.

"For sure. I don't even have a place to live right now. I don't think I can be responsible for a cat," I admit.

"Is that okay?" Wrenn looks at Heather.

"Are you kidding? I would love to! I've been thinking about getting one when I move out." Heather smiles.

"Then yes please. It almost stopped us from going, we just want to know he's happy when we're gone." Ryleigh smiles.

"Sage! We're going to be cat babysitters!" Heather looks at Sage, who looks amused by her girlfriend. Heather starts talking to Wrenn and Ryleigh about the specifics and Sage is just watching Heather. She's looking at her with this awe on her face like she can't believe that's her girlfriend.

I need to stop watching my friends be so in love with their partners. It's sickening. Gross. Except…it isn't. It's adorable and sweet. And I ache for something just as good as their love. This is why I stuck with Will for as long as I did. I didn't want to admit the truth, even to myself.

TWELVE

Harmony

When I show up at Alana's a few days later, I bring one of my favorite albums, *Girl of My Dreams* by FLETCHER. Maybe we can listen to it while I lay the new tile on the kitchen counter. That's a relatively quiet task, and I know she likes listening to records at night. I knock on the door like I always do, but this time I'm greeted by a smiling Alana.

This surprises me, considering the angry phone call I received from her mother a few days ago. Her yelling at me about not telling her where her daughter was and how I couldn't possibly be working if she was there. I sent photos of my work in progress and explained it wasn't my job to alert her to a relative staying in their house. Her husband calmed her down, apologized to me, and offered a bonus if I stayed on. I didn't have the heart to tell him I was happy to stay on either way.

"Hi." I smile.

"Hi! I'm just cleaning up. I had some friends over last night and it's a bit of a mess." Alana waves me in and shuts the door behind me.

"You saw your friends?" This surprises me.

"Yeah, I thought it was time. And I missed them so much. They made me feel a lot better about everything."

"I'm glad. I brought an album I thought you might like. Do you wanna listen to it while I work?" I ask.

"That sounds nice. I love music while I'm cleaning, it makes it feel like I'm not really working," she admits.

I pull out the album from my bag and hand it to her.

"I freaking love FLETCHER." She smiles as she takes it to the record player.

Heading to the kitchen, I can see into the living room where she's cleaning up. It's not a mess or anything, just dishes left over and a few pizza boxes. I move the tile from the boxes on the floor onto the empty counter space next to the fridge. I'm only replacing the tiles on the island today. I already removed the old tile and it's just a matter of putting the new ones down.

Alana catches my eye when she starts dancing as she picks things up. I don't think she's even thinking about it, just swaying her hips while she moves. She carries the pizza boxes outside and then comes back in. She brings the dishes over to the sink behind me and then goes back to get the rest. FLETCHER plays quietly in the background and she's humming along to the music.

"I saw her in concert a few years ago, she does an amazing show live," I tell Alana.

"I heard she usually takes her top off."

"Well, yeah she definitely did that." I blush.

"Do you go to a lot of concerts?"

"Not as much as I used to. There are too many drunk people at them. I wish there was a way to see some artists without the crowd being wasted," I admit.

"Hmm, that's true. I like seeing them sober so I can actually remember the concert the next day." Alana laughs.

"Right? We pay enough money for tickets."

"So true, my sister paid three hundred dollars to sit in the nosebleeds at a Sabrina Carpenter concert last year. But then she got wasted so I'm like, what's the point?" Alana laughs.

"Yeah, it's like, why not get drunk at home and play the album if you won't remember where you are," I add.

"Seriously!" Alana shakes her head.

"My daughter dragged me to a Wiggles concert last year, and let me say, while the people there were sober, it was the moms who were feral."

"For that purple one right?"

"How did you know?" I look at her, surprised. She doesn't have any kids.

"He's all over TikTok. He's got tattoos and he's hot," Alana admits.

"Oh, that explains it." I laugh. "I'm definitely too old for TikTok."

"How old are you?"

"I turn thirty-four in October."

"That's not even old! I turned twenty-eight and to my mother, you'd think I turned ninety-eight." Alana scoffs.

"What? Why?"

"She just acts like Will was my one chance to fall in love and get married. She made some comments about how no one else would want me now." She waves me off like it's no big deal.

"That's fucked."

Her eyes widen. "You're right. It is fucked."

"Like, I'm sorry, but that's your mother. She should be on your side."

"Are you close with your mother?" Alana asks and I wince. I guess I walked into that one.

"No. Not at all. I haven't spoken to her in over ten years."

"Oh, I'm so sorry. You just seemed like you were close."

"I know a thing or two about being a mom from Millie. I would never do what my mother did to me, to Millie. She kicked me out when I told her Jamie and I were getting married.

Wanted nothing to do with me and then we never spoke again," I explain.

"I'm genuinely so sorry. I don't have the best relationship with my mother, but that's not something anyone should have to go through." Alana places her palm on my shoulder. I can feel the heat radiating from her skin.

The song changes to "Better Version" by FLETCHER, and I put my hand over hers. "Dance with me."

"Dance with you?" She looks surprised. I'll never get used to her looking like I'm asking her something crazy when in reality, it's something that should be expected.

"Yeah, come on. Dance with me." I take her hand in mine, and she follows me to the living room.

The music is louder there, and she's moved some of the furniture because there's more space to move. I can't tell what's missing, but it leaves space for us. Alana follows my lead, and I relax as her hands wrap around my neck. She's only a few inches shorter than me so we seem to fit together perfectly. I put my hands on her waist and we both sway together gently. The music is playing but the only thing I can hear is the sound of my heart beating out of my chest. I wonder if it's ever beat that fast before and if Alana can hear it. She doesn't let on if she can.

I can smell the scent of vanilla shampoo, her hair piled in a messy bun on the top of her head. It's tilted to the side, curls slipping from it all around her. Her dark, warm eyes gaze into mine for just a second before looking away. She blushes and I smile.

"I don't think I've ever slow danced with another woman before," she admits, looking up at me.

"Is it different than dancing with a man?"

"No, not much. You're more muscular than Will, if I'm being honest." She laughs.

"I knew I caught you checking me out that day!" I laugh. She had been all but drooling when I was outside. I had even flexed a bit for her.

"Oh, God. I didn't think you noticed!" She buries her head in my chest with a laugh.

I tilt her chin up with my thumb and make her look at me. Her cheeks are a bright pink and her dark eyelashes flutter at me. "I always notice you."

She blushes even harder, but I don't allow her to look away. I just want to capture this moment. I keep holding her chin steady. Her pouty lips beg to be kissed. I know this time she wouldn't taste like wine. I know she wants this as much as I want it. But I also know we can't, not yet. I'm about to drop her chin when I hear the door slam.

"What the hell is going on here?!" A male's voice causes us to break apart.

I pull Alana behind me instinctively. I don't know who the hell this is but I'm not taking any chances. He's standing there with his phone in hand, dressed in business attire and his blond hair perfectly gelled. He's at least 6'4" but I think I could probably take him if I needed to. I'm about to ask who the hell he thinks he is when Alana speaks, peeking out behind me.

"Will?" she says quietly.

"Will?" I mumble. *Her ex-fiancé?* What the fuck is he doing here?

"It's okay, Harmony, this is my...this is Will." She sighs. I don't let go of her waist and she doesn't ask me to either.

"Who the hell is this?" Will yells.

I can understand his anger now. He just caught his ex-fiancée about to possibly kiss someone. I'd be pissed as hell too. I try to explain.

"Look—"

He cuts me off. "No, I'm not fucking talking to you."

"Will," Alana says warningly.

"I find out you've been hiding out for weeks. Is this why? Did you fucking cheat on me?"

"I-I should go," I decide. This was not my business, and I don't want to be in the middle of this.

"I didn't cheat on you," Alana says quietly. She almost shrinks being near him. "I'm sorry." She doesn't look at me as she says it.

I have to walk past Will on the way out, but he doesn't give me a second look. His eyes are angrily focused on Alana, who is silent across the room. I slip out the front door and drive as far away as I possibly can. I hate the way Alana was shrinking in front of him, but I know I couldn't stay and watch it. It also isn't my place to try and intervene. It's too much drama that doesn't involve me. If she was my girlfriend, I would've stood up for her, but she and I aren't anything. He's a man who is rightfully upset. If she had left me at the altar, I would've been upset with her too.

I pull into my driveway, and I relax a bit. I wish I had a way to check up on her. Would she be okay later? But I stop, it wasn't my job to save everyone. She has friends she can and probably will talk to about this. She'll handle it the way she wants to, and it wasn't my place to worry about it. I know he isn't dangerous. Alana didn't run away because he was abusive or something, she ran away because she didn't love him. It's nothing she can't handle. As long as she stands up for herself and doesn't let herself shrink for him. She's so powerful and strong, if only she could see it. I don't understand why it took her wedding day for her to run away from him, but seeing her in front of him now, I understand it.

For some reason, she feels small around him. He makes her feel like she isn't the powerful woman I see her as. He's taken so much from her; I don't think she realizes the extent of it. I know she only told me a crumb of what happened between the two of them. They were together for years, she almost married him, so I know there was more she hadn't brought up yet. But I also know I can't do anything so I tried to push it from my mind. Too often I try to control things as a fake sense of control, but in reality, there is very little in this life we can control.

I hope Alana stands up to him once and for all. For her sake more than mine. She deserves to tell him what she told me about how she feels. Maybe it won't change anything for him, but at least she'll get it off her chest.

THIRTEEN

Alana

"How did you know I'm here?" I ask. Harmony slipped out before I could say anything more to her, and I was thrown off by seeing Will here. This had been my escape, my safe house, and I feel like I'm suddenly under attack.

"Your mother told me. She said she came to see you and thought I might be interested in knowing where you are." He clenches his fists. "Do you know how fucking embarrassing it was to be left at the freaking altar?"

"I'm sorry—"

He cuts me off. "No. You fucking left me in front of all our friends and family. How the hell was I supposed to publicly move on from that? You've made me look unstable to the company. I've been doing damage control for *weeks* trying to get the board back on my side." He growls.

The board? That's what this was about? He wasn't upset that I left him, he was upset about how me leaving him made him *look*. Something snaps in me.

"You're fucking kidding me, right?" I talk over him.

"What?" I've thrown him off guard. He's told me too many times that I shouldn't curse, and it wasn't *ladylike*, but fuck that.

"You're fucking joking right? You're not seriously here yelling at me about how it made you *look bad* and not about the fact that I left your ass?"

"Of course I'm upset about that too." He scoffs. And there it is. Like always, I'm an afterthought to him. He was upset about losing me because it didn't benefit him.

"I was going to fucking apologize to you, but fuck that. I'm not sorry. I'm only sorry I didn't do it sooner." I cross my arms.

"Alana, seriously with the cursing, it's not necessary or ladylike." He rolls his eyes.

"I'm sorry. I don't give a *fuck*." I smirk, waiting for him to give me a hard time.

"You were always like this. I thought we'd gotten past this *wild streak* of yours. Always pushing buttons and being so much. It's enough, I was going to marry you despite all of that but maybe you did us both a favor." He says *wild streak* the same way you'd turn your nose up at a dirty diaper.

I'm taken aback by his words, but I don't let them affect me right now. There will be time for that later. Right now is my time to stand up for myself. For the first time in our relationship, I'm not going to be a people pleaser and agree with him.

"It's not a wild streak. It's called speaking my fucking mind. I'm so sick of agreeing with you because it's easier. You and I were never going to fucking work because you never really loved me. You loved the idea of me, my family, and that I listened for the most part. But I'm not that same woman anymore. I don't want to be a little people pleaser anymore."

His face drops, like he isn't used to me talking back to him. He's processing his next thought. Like he isn't sure how to win this. I'm sure this is going exactly the opposite of how he expected this to go. He probably thought I had cold feet and that I'd want to come home to him if he asked nicely.

"I want my ring back, and I want your shit out of my house," he says angrily.

I don't know if that's supposed to upset me, but it doesn't. "Sounds good, I'll send my sister and Gemma over to collect my things."

Looking down at my engagement ring, I forgot I was even still wearing it. I haven't taken it off, but it wasn't on purpose. I've been wearing it for so long at this point that it was more of a routine than it wasn't. It wasn't my style at all. I had hinted for months, even going ring shopping with him, explaining how I liked silver jewelry and a smaller diamond. Instead, he gave me the biggest square cut diamond he could fit on my finger that constantly got caught on everything. I slide the ring off my finger and toss it at him. He doesn't catch it, not having an athletic bone in his body. He bends down to pick it up.

"I hope you know all you lost."

"The only thing I know I lost is not having to be sexually unsatisfied for the rest of my life." I laugh.

"You're such a child. Of course you'd bring sex into this. At least I can tell everyone how you were cheating on me this whole time." He says it like a threat. Part of me wants to stop him but instead I shrug.

"Tell people what you want. I know I didn't cheat on you, but you can believe whatever lies you want."

"I'm seriously shocked I ever thought I wanted to marry you."

"The feeling's mutual."

I move to help him out the front door. I don't need to entertain this any further. The only thing I want to do is get him out of here. And maybe burn some sage throughout the house.

"Bye." I shove him out the front door and lock it behind him.

He's yelling something but I walk over to the record player, pop in my Olivia Rodrigo album, and raise the volume all the way up. I scream the lyrics as loud as I can and dance around the living room. I'm free. My hand feels lighter without that gaudy diamond on my finger. Tears fall from my eyes, but I think they're happy tears. I've never felt better than I do in this moment. I close my eyes and let them fall as I dance around the room. I don't know how long I'm dancing and singing until the record stops. The silence shows me that Will is gone, and I don't have to worry about him anymore.

I finish the dishes I was going to do earlier, then I look for my phone. Now that I've faced the worst of it, I know I could turn it back on for good. The first thing I do is clear all my messages. I'm starting fresh and the last thing I need is to see something about the wedding. The second thing I do is block Will's number. I don't need to hear from him; in fact, I don't want anything to do with him anymore.

Wrenn's the first one to notice me typing in the group chat.

Wrenn: IS THAT MY SISTER TYPING?!
Heather: How the frick did you notice that?
Kim: Is she back?
Me: Y'all act like I was dead
Wrenn: It's sort of like you were!
Me: I'm back! Will came to talk and let's just say I sent his ass packing
Kim: What do those emojis mean?
Me: Me closing the door on him lol
* Gemma, Wrenn & Kim loved your message *
Gemma: Thank the Lord. I will not miss his nasty ass.
* Wrenn loved your message *
* Me, Kim & Heather laughed at your message *
Ryleigh: I couldn't find my phone, but Wrenn is laughing, what's happening?
Me: I'm back, I even blocked Will
Ryleigh: hallelujah!

. . .

I bring the phone with me and plug it in next to my bed. I wish I had Harmony's number. I'd love to send her a text and let her know Will is gone. I didn't know if she'd come back over tonight, but at least she'd know I handled it. I'm glad she left so she wasn't in the middle of everything. That was something I needed to do on my own. She isn't coming over again until tomorrow night according to the schedule. And I'm sure she'll be more cautious about almost kissing me if she thinks my ex is going to walk in.

Feeling jittery, I decide to pull out the journal Norah got me and write an entry.

I always thought I wanted the picture-perfect life. The ease of being with someone who worked and had tons of money. Two children and be a stay-at-home mom while they grew up. My life was going according to plan until the day of my wedding. It was like, as soon as I was going to be handed everything I wanted, I realized it wasn't my dream. It was ideals my family had put on me and imbedded in me, but it wasn't what I actually wanted.

My mother may never forgive me for running out on Will, and that's okay. But at least I know wherever I end up and whoever I end up with, I'll be happy.

Tonight, I stood up to a man who took everything from me. He may not have hit me or abused me, but he took so many little things from me until I didn't recognize myself. I was so complacent and such a people pleaser that I didn't bother stopping myself from settling. I should've realized it sooner. I wish I had listened the many, many times my friends brought it up to me. But it's probably better that I figured it out myself.

I also slow danced with a woman tonight. And it felt more natural than it ever was being with Will. I could feel her heart beating against my chest. Our passion and tension were palpable. Both of us wanting to make a move but terrified of the other.

She made me feel alive. I was slowly getting to know her and every time we spoke, I felt even safer to be myself around her. At first, I thought it was because she was a woman. We were only going to be friends, my guard was down. But now that I've admitted my attraction for her I know that it's because of her.

I don't know what might happen with her, if anything. Maybe nothing. But at least I know that I could be myself with someone and they would want to be with me. They wouldn't try to change me or belittle me into being something different.

I fall back into bed, closing my eyes, and remember the way Harmony's body felt perfectly against mine. It wasn't sexual, but intimate. I felt safe dancing with her. Listening to her heart. Accidentally admitting that I'm attracted to her. It felt easy, simple, with her. There were no hoops I needed to jump through or task I needed to accomplish to prove myself. She didn't expect anything from me. She didn't want anything from me. And yeah, maybe that will change in time, but it seems more likely that she just wants me. She wants to get to know me and she definitely wants to fuck me. She just has way more self-control than I do.

I text my sister and Gemma, asking if they can pick up my stuff from Will's this week when he's at work. I picked them because I know they'd give him more sass than he thought was possible if he tried to say something about me. They've been dying for a chance to put him in his place. I don't think he'd be stupid enough to walk into that, but then again, there's a time for everything. They had both been so patient with him, when he never gave them any reason to be. So this was like my gift to them. They both text back immediately accepting, Wrenn being less obvious with her reply.

Wrenn: Fuck yes, I hate that guy. Lemme get a chance to hit him.

Gemma: Sounds good, maybe he'll say something stupid, and I can call him an asshat.

. . .

I laugh. They both look out for me. I know they have my best interest at heart. Even now, I'm sure they'd pack everything up and put something smelly in his vents. Something that wouldn't get them into too much trouble legally.

FOURTEEN

Harmony

"You can ask, you know. You look like you're going to explode." Alana chuckles.

"I don't want to bother you, but I am curious," I admit. I'm working on the tile I couldn't get done yesterday, and Alana seems to be in a chipper mood, but neither of us talked about the elephant in the room.

"You're not a bother. I just didn't know if you cared." She shrugs. Putting down her book, she gets off the couch and walks into the kitchen.

"Of course, I care. So what happened when I left?"

"He yelled and told me I was missing the best thing that would ever happen to me. So I laughed and basically told him to suck my dick. He asked for the ring back and I happily threw it at him. And then I pushed him out the door. He started yelling but I turned on the music and danced until he was gone." She has a smug smile on her face.

"Holy shit. You told him off?"

"Of fucking course, I did. He didn't even care that I left him, he was more concerned by the optics of it." She rolls her eyes.

"What a prick."

"I know. So I turned back on my phone and blocked his ass.

But it also made me realize I don't have your number." She bats her eyes at me. Fuck, I go weak in the knees when she does that.

"I gave it to you on my business card." I furrow my brow.

"Oh yeah!" She smacks her forehead. "How did I forget that?"

"Well here, let me put it in." I put my hand out and she hands me her phone. I type in my name and number before saving it.

"Thanks." She smiles before slipping it in her back pocket.

I keep working on laying the tile. It's fairly simple to do, and I thank God I remembered to close the glue cap yesterday or it would be shit today. Alana hops on the kitchen counter behind me and swings her legs slowly. I smirk to myself when I feel her eyes on my ass. I make a point to bend over a little further so she can get a better angle. It's clear this woman has never checked out another woman before because she's way too obvious about it. Men wouldn't pick up on it, but when you check out a woman, you wanna be a tad bit more subtle.

"See something you like?" I turn around, catching her chewing on her bottom lip.

"I, uh, was just watching you work," she lies, her face giving her up.

"Sure, you were." I chuckle.

She's about to defend herself when there's a huge boom from the kitchen window. Alana jumps off the counter toward me and I glance out the window. Dark clouds that weren't there an hour ago are slowly getting closer to the house. As I look at the clouds, it starts raining. It goes from dry to pouring showers in a matter of seconds. Alana clutches to my side as the thunder hits again. I wrap my arm around her side, and she seems to relax.

"I wasn't expecting a storm like this." I frown.

"I can't say I've checked the weather recently," Alana says.

"If it's okay with you, I can finish this up first thing in the morning, but I should get home." I sigh.

"Do you have your daughter tonight? Millie?" Alana looks at me with wide eyes.

"Uh, no? Why?" I look at her confused.

"You could stay the night." My face changes from confused to surprised. "In the spare bedroom! We have a spare room! Four actually!"

"Oh, you don't have to—"

Alana cuts me off. "Look, I'm terrified of thunder and lightning, okay? And I'd just feel safer if you stayed the night. If you can."

"Are you sure? I don't want to be in the way."

"You aren't. I swear we have extra bedrooms, and it's not some ploy to like, jump your bones or something. I just don't want to be alone." She sighs.

I think about it for a moment before answering, "Okay."

"Really?" Her eyes light up.

"Yeah, it came out of nowhere so the roads will be shit until the morning anyway. It'll probably be safer if I stayed here." I shrug.

"Thank you." Alana hugs me and then runs away. "I'm going to make up the bed!"

I don't know if it's the best idea, staying alone with her in the house. But at least we'll be in different beds. It isn't like we have zero self-control. It's just been too freaking long since I've gotten laid. I finish up on the tile and then clear out the boxes. I've been putting them in the garage until garbage day so they wouldn't be in the way. I look at the to do list for the rest of this job. I only need to do the trims on the kitchen island, install the new windows in the bathroom, and exchange the shower head in the bathroom to the one that matches the others. I'd probably be done by the end of the week, which leaves me with a stinging in my gut.

I take a few hits of my vape, not wanting to stand in the rain and hoping Alana wouldn't be upset at me for doing it in the garage. If I'm going to be spending the night, I'll need a few more to get me through it.

"Ahh!" Alana comes back into the room with a blanket

wrapped around her. Another strike of lightning hits, making her scream.

"You okay?"

"It's so stupid. I know I'm a grown up. I should be over this by now." She frowns.

Is that what Will said to her? What a fucking prick. "It's normal for adults to have fears. I'm terrified of snakes."

"Snakes? Really?" Alana cracks a smile.

"Hey! This is a safe space," I tease.

"Right, okay. Go on." Alana smiles.

"I was seven, and my mom took me on a hike. Let me also preface this by saying, I ate a shit ton of jellybeans. I think it was around Easter or something. But anyway, we're hiking, and my stomach starts to hurt. It got worse and worse, but I didn't say anything and of course I didn't look. So I didn't see it and I threw up on the snake. Which, of course, pissed off the snake, so I had to climb into a tree until my mom caught the snake on a stick and threw it into a river."

"Oh, my God." Alana is choking back laughter.

"It's fine, you can laugh." I smile. "But that's why I no longer eat jellybeans or like snakes."

"That's too good." She's cracking up, and I smile at her.

"I love your laugh." It slips out before I can think and not talk out of my ass. Or maybe this is my pussy, since I'm not thinking clearly.

"Thanks." Alana blushes.

"What do you say we make some dinner and watch a movie? I'm off the clock for the day and I can use something to eat," I suggest.

"Okay." Alana nods and I follow her to the kitchen. "I have some chicken I could cook, or…"

I move next to her to see in the fridge and her voice gets shaky. It seems my presence has that effect on her. "What about a tried-and-true favorite?" I say, pulling out some ingredients.

"Mac and cheese?" she guesses.

"Yup, you have exactly what I need to make my three cheese mac. It's Millie's favorite." I smile.

"I love it. Do you need any help?"

"Nope. Just sit back and watch me work."

I start boiling a little bit of water to cook the noodles. She doesn't have elbows, but any shape of pasta will work. Millie usually prefers the wheels anyway. I grab some flour, milk, three types of cheeses, and butter. I add salt and pepper for a little taste and begin cooking. Alana sits back on the counter and watches me work. Every so often the thunder booms again, and I count the time in-between each one. It's getting closer, but I didn't want to tell Alana that. I'm also worried about losing power. I don't know how much time we have, so I move a little quicker than normal. I scoop a few spoonfuls into two bowls, and it's steaming while Alana takes a bite.

"Ow! Fuck!" She groans.

"It just came off the stove! Of course it's hot!" I laugh.

"It just looked so good! I didn't think it would be that hot." She pouts.

"Here." I hand her a glass of cold water and she sips it.

"Thanks." She puts it down before blowing on another spoonful and having some. "Oh, my God. This is delicious!" She lets out a moan, and my eyes go wide.

I'm speechless as she takes another bite and lets out another gracious moan. This woman is going to be the death of me. I can feel myself getting wet just listening to her. It sounds awfully similar to that day I heard her in the shower. Would she make those same sounds with me? I try to push the thought from my mind, but I'm already there.

"Aren't you hungry? Have some!" Alana is oblivious to my staring.

I force myself to have a bite and make sure I don't choke on it. The last thing I need is for her to touch me right now. She's too busy in her food coma to notice, but the thunder is getting closer. I pack up the food in a container and dump the dishes in the sink. I'll worry about them later. As a new strike of lightning hits outside, and the power jumps. All the lights flicker, and Alana's eyes go wide.

"Oh shit, do you think we're going to lose power?" She gets off the counter and looks out the window.

"It's...it's probably possible." I tread lightly. I don't know the extent of her fears.

"Okay." She takes a deep breath.

"Why don't we finish eating and then worry about it if it happens?" I suggest.

"Yeah, okay sure." She nods.

Alana takes a few more bites of the mac and cheese but gone is her happy mood. She's teetering on anxious now that the weather is worse. I wish I had something more comforting to say but I don't know what. The thunder booms again outside, and three seconds later, the lightning strikes. The next time it's even closer, and then the lightning strikes with no thunder and the power flicks off. I wait for a moment, thinking maybe it'll come back on. But as the storm continues on outside, the power stays off. It's quiet now, all the air conditioners winding down with no power. All we can hear is the pounding rain on the roof and the thunder.

"Sh-should we do anything? I don't think I've ever been here alone without power," Alana admits shakily.

"The windows are safe. I'd say we need to stay away from water, so no showers or doing dishes right now. It might get hot without the air conditioners but there isn't much we can do about that. Were they on in the bedrooms?"

"Yeah, I turned yours on, too."

"Okay, let's go shut the doors so the cool air stays in as much as possible." I try to think of anything else we might need to do. "Do you think there are candles somewhere?"

"We definitely have matches. Maybe there's candles in the bedrooms?" Alana says.

"Okay. Why don't we go check?"

It's clear Alana doesn't want to go by herself, so I follow her to the bedrooms, shutting the doors behind us after we look for candles. I pull my phone out of my pocket and send a quick text to Jamie. I let her know I'm safe and ask if they're okay. Jamie texts back a few minutes later saying they lost power, so she'll be conserving her phone battery, but Millie is asleep and she's okay. I ask her to let me know if she needs anything or if anything changes. I know there isn't much I can do from here, but I want to at least make sure they are okay.

FIFTEEN

Alana

Harmony helps me look for candles in the bedrooms, but we don't see anything, so we head back to the kitchen. I'm a little shaky from the thunder and lightning. Now that the power is out, I'm even more relieved I asked Harmony to spend the night. It's selfish of me, but I know I don't want to be here by myself tonight. If the power had gone out and I was here alone, I would've crawled under my bed and hid until it came back on.

Harmony starts looking through the kitchen drawers for candles and matches. I help by staying away from the window and out of her way. She finds the matches and puts them on the counter she finished working on today. And at the last drawer in the kitchen, she gasps, holding up the candles happily. It's dark in here but I can see her face in the moonlight and the light from the intermittent lightning.

She begins lighting them, spreading them around the kitchen. They're small tea lights and she found an entire bag of them, but she's careful not to use too many at once. Once she lights a few, she smiles at me.

"Feeling a little better?" she asks.

"Yeah, I'm sorry." I sigh. I wish I wasn't such a scaredy cat.

"You have to stop apologizing. If I saw a snake in here, I'd be running for the hills." She laughs.

"Thank you for staying tonight. I was worried you'd say no."

"I'm glad you asked me."

She moves closer, standing next to me now. I ease a bit, knowing she's close. It's like she can control my emotions just by being near me. She's making sure I'm okay. I look up at her, light blue eyes twinkling in the light. The flame dances across her eyes. I feel a shiver run down my back and I know it can't be the AC. I had been starting to feel hot, but now I'm not sure what I'm feeling. Harmony swallows and I let out a deep breath. Is she feeling this too? We're both so quiet.

She moves closer. This time, her face is just inches from mine as my back presses into the kitchen counter. She leans against me, her thin body towering over me, suddenly making me feel small. We were only inches apart, but the way she makes me feel... My breath hitches as I can feel her breath only inches from mine. Is this really about to happen? Is she really about to kiss me? Then she closes the distance, and her lips fall into mine. I'm putty under her touch, and as her hard, sculpted body leans into mine, I know I'm a goner. I spread my legs just a little for her to stand between them. The cool tile hits the bare skin on my back and her hands reach for my waist. I can feel her fingertips brushing slightly on my stomach. Our tongues tangle together like they never want to be apart.

A soft moan escapes my lips and falls into her. I'm drunk off her lips and when she pulls away, I feel dizzy. Like a kiss can't be that good, sober. She presses her lips to mine again, once, making sure this is okay. A slight nod of my head is all she needs. Her hands loop around the belt loops of my jeans, and when she pulls me in even closer, I lose my breath. I run my hand down her sculpted chest. Her small breasts, her hard abs, stopping at her tattooed hip bone. Fuck. I'd noticed it earlier when her shirt rode up and her jeans were hanging low.

In this moment, I no longer want to take anything slow. I

want to take this moment as far as it will go. My breasts press against hers, nipples pebbling tightly as her hand slides up my body, stopping to grab my breast and squeeze. With my nipple between her thumb and forefinger, I bite down on her bottom lip involuntarily. Her hand continues moving up, sliding on my neck to the back of my head. Her hand steadies me. She slips her fingers through my curls and tilts my head back. She's gripping my neck, and I look at her and her bright blue eyes. Fuck. My panties are a puddle in my jeans. If this isn't going any further, at least I'll have material to get off to.

I haven't been able to use my vibrator in weeks. It isn't like I can ask any of my friends to sneak into Will's house and get it. They're collecting my things from him this week, but I don't even know where I left it. I hid it so often to keep Will from getting mad that I probably hid it somewhere obscure. So any material I can use to get me off faster would be amazing. Harmony is already a walking wet dream. My friends only confirmed that when they saw her Instagram.

Harmony grips her hand around my throat and pulls me back so she can look at me. Fuck, I'm unable to form any words as she looks at me. Her sharp jawline brushes against my neck as she leaves kisses from my earlobe to my collarbone. God. Is this what real passion feels like? Sex with Will never felt like this, and Harmony and I were only kissing.

"I've been dying to do this," she admits.

"Mmm, me too," I mumble. Her tongue is still touching my neck. I can feel the buzz of this all the way to my toes.

All of a sudden, she loosens her grip on my neck and grabs my hips, picking me up and placing me on the edge of the counter. I open my legs wide enough for her to fit between them before wrapping them around her. Her mouth immediately matches mine, and I run my fingers through her short hair. It's softer than I thought with the sides tickling my hand more than the longer curls.

I can feel her hips bumping into my center. Just a small

brush, her hips bucking against mine. Her mouth is on my ear, tugging my earlobe between her teeth. Her hand slides down my back and she grips my ass with two hands, holding me closer to her body. I tilt my head back. I'm shivering in anticipation of what she might touch next. I was like a firecracker, ready to explode at any second.

"You're so sexy, do you know that?" she murmurs in my ear.

"Says the walking wet dream," I mumble.

"Excuse me?" She wiggles her brow, pulling back to look at me.

"You're so hot. My friends saw you and couldn't believe how hot you are."

"Your friends saw me?" She smirks. Of course she would find this amusing.

"Less talking, more kissing." I try to kiss her, but she holds a firm grip on the back of my hair, and I groan. Why the fuck did that turn me on so much?

"No. Tell me why your friends saw a picture of me."

"I might have told them about you. How I was, well *am*, attracted to you." I try to look away, but it's hard when someone's holding you hostage.

Harmony fucking laughs. And I blush because I'm embarrassed about everything. I don't know what the hell I'm doing.

"I've never been with a woman before," I admit.

Harmony's eyes soften as she brushes a piece of hair from my face. "We can go as slow as you need."

"I don't want slow. I just want you to show me the ropes." She looks at me with desire as she moans. Like something out of a freaking porno. God, she couldn't get any hotter.

"As much as I'd love to eat you out on the kitchen counter, I think it might be better to move this to the couch. I'm not having sex with you tonight."

"You're not?" I furrow my brow. Isn't that what she wants?

"Before you get in your head about it, trust me, it's not that I don't want to. I'm so wet—it's a slip and slide down there.

But I don't wanna rush anything with you," Harmony says softly.

"Okay."

I was about to be a little hurt, thinking she didn't want me in that way. But the fact that she knew enough to reassure me and that she doesn't want to rush anything? This is completely new to me. I can't recall a time someone delayed sleeping with me. If the offer was there, no one's ever told me to wait before. I'm taken aback but also flattered. I want to be with her. But she's right, there is no need for us to rush anything. It's not like either of us is going anywhere.

"Why don't we move to the couch? There might be a little more room for this." Harmony holds out her hand, and I follow her to the living room.

She goes back to grab a few of the candles as I sit on one of the couches, moving the pillows out of the way.

"Is there, like, a base you want to stop at? I don't think I've just kissed someone since I was in high school," I admit.

"We should definitely keep our pants on, but everything else seems okay. Does that seem right?"

"Yeah." I try to sound casual, but I probably look as turned on as I feel.

Harmony sits next to me and pulls me in for a kiss. I climb onto her lap, my legs straddling her. I've never made out with a woman before, but fuck. They are so much easier to be on top of, and so much hotter too. Harmony seems to know exactly what I like even though it's nothing I've experienced before. She pulls my hips down to hers, grabbing my ass tightly in her hands.

"I've been dying to get a piece of this," she murmurs against my lips.

Her dirty talk isn't making it any easier to not fuck her tonight. I slide my hands down her chest, reaching her breasts, and she moans softly. Her thin T-shirt with some funny saying is a barrier between us. I breathe slowly as I take her breasts in my hands. I can feel her nipples hardening through her shirt.

Which is when she grabs my hips, scoops me up, and plops me onto the couch. She climbs on top of me, kissing my lips. I close my eyes as she nibbles on my earlobe again. Her warm breath invites me to beg for more. I chew on my bottom lip, desperately trying not to sound as desperate for this as I feel. She slides my shirt up my stomach and bends down to leave me kisses. She presses her lips against my hip bone, and I shiver. My fingers grip the fabric of the couch. Then she presses a kiss to my belly button, and I moan, not giving a fuck if I come off as needy. I *am* needy, and I need this.

She kisses further up until she slides the shirt over my breasts. Both my nipples are hard, the cool air hitting them even though there is no actual cool air in here. I'm starting to sweat from the AC being off but I don't care. Harmony lightly tugs on my nipple with her teeth, and I moan.

"I've never heard a better sound." She smirks proudly before kissing me again.

I hold her face in my hands, soft skin and even softer lips. She moves her hips against mine, and I let her press her body into me. Both of us radiate enough heat to start a fire. Both of us want more and more, but we know this will be worth the wait.

SIXTEEN

Harmony

Alana and I spend the night bordering the line between making out and getting off. A few times, I'm sure she's close to coming even though she still has her pants on. I'd be lying if I said I wasn't close, too. But at some point, we make our way to our separate bedrooms, and I leave a lingering kiss on her lips. I make sure all the candles are blown out, and I tug off my jeans before sliding in the bed. My panties are sticking to my pussy because I'm so wet. I don't want to, but there is no way I can sleep when I feel this wired.

So I slip my hand down my panties and bite back a moan when I feel how wet I am. My fingers could literally slip and slide down there. They glaze across my clit, the bundle of nerves begging to explode. Closing my eyes, all I see is Alana. Her beautiful dark hair, her pouty pink lips, and the blush that stays on her face when I tell her all the dirty things I want to do to her. But it's her moans that I've tried to commit to memory that gets me going. I slide two fingers inside, wanting to speed this up. The last thing I want is to get caught.

I curl my fingers inside myself and let my thumb coated in my wetness brush across my clit. A few pumps of my fingers and I can already feel my orgasm building. I knew it wasn't going to take much. Not after how much foreplay Alana and I had. I could've kept kissing her, but we both got tired and my jaw started to hurt. Imagine kissing someone for so long that your jaw gets sore. I press down hard on my clit and cover my mouth with my free hand. Closing my eyes, I see literal stars as I come. Riding it out, I pull out my hand and run to the bathroom to wash them.

Out of habit, I flick on a bathroom light, and to my surprise, the light comes back on. The power must be back. To make sure it isn't a fluke, I wash my hands and head back to the bedroom to see if the light in there works. When it does, I go to knock on Alana's door. She answers with a yawn.

Her eyes go wide as she looks at me. "Well, if you're going to knock on my door looking like that, I might become a morning person."

It's my turn to blush. In my excitement about the power, I forgot to put on a pair of pants. "The power is back on," I say, ignoring her.

"Oh, thank God! I was sweating bullets in here." Alana walks back into the room and turns the AC on. It roars to life, and she smiles.

"I thought you'd like to know, I'll see you in the morning." I smile. Alana presses her lips to mine for a quick kiss before I head back to the other bedroom.

I turn on the AC in there, relieved I have some air. I can't fall asleep if I'm too hot, and it's definitely too hot in here. I fall asleep once it gets cool enough.

In the morning, Alana is awake first. I can hear her playing music quietly in the kitchen. After going to pee and swiping some toothpaste over my teeth with my finger, I check my phone for any update from Jamie. She got her power back shortly after we did, and Millie woke up having no clue it was ever out. There's no update after that so I head into the kitchen, this time with pants, on and find Alana singing into the spatula. She's wearing these tiny pajama shorts that barely cover her ass, showing off a bit of cheek with each sway of her hips.

"Good morning." I smile.

"Oh, my goodness! You have to stop doing that." She clutches her chest.

"Sorry, you looked so cute dancing." I smirk.

"I was trying to make us some breakfast." She rolls her eyes.

I peek over her shoulder. She's making pancakes, eggs, and bacon. "It looks delicious."

She leans in to kiss me but I back away. "I have morning breath!"

"I smell toothpaste." She narrows her eyes.

"I only did what I could, I didn't have a toothbrush."

She leans in again and this time I kiss her chastely. She grumbles, going back to cooking. I stand back watching, waiting to see if she needs any help with anything.

"Did you sleep okay?" she asks.

"I did, how about you?"

"Better than most nights. I was actually tired for once." She laughs.

"Do you usually have trouble sleeping?"

"More like staying asleep. Or falling asleep to start. I'm usually not tired enough lately," she admits.

"I don't want this to come across as rude, but do you work? Or have a job?"

Alana laughs. "It's not rude. I probably look like an heiress. I do have a job; I'm an interior designer. But I took the entire month off from projects, I thought I'd be on my honeymoon and then recovering from the wedding planning."

"That makes sense. I didn't know if you were between jobs at the moment or something."

"Nope, I just needed some time off. Which I'm happy to

finally be taking. I'm not sure what I'm going to do when I get back to work."

"Are you thinking of changing careers or something?"

"No. I just wonder if there's more I can be doing to bring me joy. I was taking on a lot of high-profile clients but truthfully, their homes are so boring. Everything is white and expensive and breakable. I just want to have fun with color every once in a while."

Alana places a plate of food in front of me on the counter and gets one for herself. She waves me into the living room and we both sit on opposite couches so we can face the other.

"You want to find joy again."

"What?"

"In your work, you're looking for things to bring you joy," I explain.

"Yes. I just wish I could choose some smaller clients with a more fun job." She shrugs as she eats.

"Well, why can't you?"

Alana opens her mouth, then closes it with a frown. "I guess I could. I never really thought about it before."

"Do you want to go on a date with me?" I ask.

Alana's mouth drops open, almost losing the piece of bacon she was chewing on. "W-what?"

"A date? Would you want to go on one?"

"I- Yes. Yes, I would." She smiles, her cheeks turning red.

"Good, after breakfast we can go out," I decide.

"Today?" Her eyes widen.

"I don't see why not, unless you're busy or something."

"Okay, you're right." She nods.

"Go get dressed, but we're stopping at my apartment so I can brush my teeth and change my clothes." I tell her.

"That's fair. Where are we going?"

"It's a surprise."

"Okay." She makes a face like she wants to complain but instead she agrees.

Once we're done eating, Alana disappears to go get dressed. She comes back out in a pair of jeans and a crop top. I make sure to open the door for her as we get into my car, and I plug the route into the GPS. I don't know my way around town yet. Alana waits in the car while I go in to change, brush my teeth for real, and spend five minutes vaping. I'm working on not vaping anymore since I know the smell bothers Alana, but I'm not able to go cold turkey. So I hit it a few times before I go back to the car.

"We're going bowling! I don't think I've been since I was, like, fifteen." She smiles.

"Is that a good or bad thing?" I raise an eyebrow.

"I mean, it sounds like fun. My friends and I never go anymore, but when we were teenagers, it was one of the only places that would let us hang out for hours and hours."

"I've taken Millie to this one. I like looking for different things to do. I get bored of going to the park over and over or just staying inside," I explain.

"I'm the same way! I love finding new places to go." She smiles.

When we get there, I pay for two hours of unlimited bowling and our shoes. We get lane number thirteen and head to the end. It's right by the food counter so we instantly smell the French fries and hot dogs cooking. We aren't even hungry, but smelling that makes my stomach growl.

"We have to get some fries," Alana says reading my mind.

"For sure. You put in our names, and I'll go get some." I kiss her cheek before heading to the food counter.

As I order the fries, I think about what I just did. Am I allowed to kiss her in public? We haven't really talked about it yet. I mean, this is our first date. She didn't flinch or pull away, but I don't want to cross any lines. I'll have to ask her when I get back with the fries. I don't know if she's a PDA type of girl or not.

"Hot fries for a hot girl," I say placing the fries on the table by our lane.

"Ooo, yum!" Alana races over and takes two, dipping them in ketchup and shoving them in her mouth.

"Was it okay that I kissed you before?"

"Huh?" She mumbles, the fries in her mouth.

"Like, I should've asked. But PDA is that cool or not?"

Alana smiles, swallows before answering, "Any type of PDA from you is okay. I'm a fan."

"Good." My stomach does a little flip. The urge to kiss her on the mouth only grows bigger.

I bowl first, grabbing the eleven-pound ball. Throwing it straight down the middle, I hit six of the ten pins before the ball goes down. I get my second chance, and of course I get a gutter ball. Groaning, I head back to Alana and the fries.

"My turn!" she sings, grabbing a red, twelve-pound ball.

She stands with her legs wide, swings the ball between them, and rolls it down the lane. To my surprise, she gets a strike. All the pins get picked up and she cheers. I thought I'd be the one to impress her, my time with Millie finally paying off skills-wise. But it seems like maybe she is going to teach me a thing or two.

We go back and forth for a bit until the fries are gone. Then we both stick by the ball return. Maybe I need to get a heavier ball. So far, she is kicking my ass ninety-six to thirty-seven. I pick up her ball instead of mine.

"Are you stealing my ball?"

"I thought it might help, considering how bad I'm losing."

"I can give you some pointers if you want." She winks.

"No thanks, I think I can handle this."

Alana laughs, watching me as I bowl with her ball. Which immediately falls into the gutter, and I groan, throwing my hands in the air.

"You've got to be kidding me!"

"Are you sure you don't want any help?" She giggles.

"No." I glare at her. I'm too competitive now.

I use my second chance to try and really focus when Alana comes up behind me. "You're too close to the lane, take a few steps back and try."

Figuring I have nothing to lose, I backup and try again. This time, the ball hits all ten pins at once. Alana is holding back her laughter. So I walk over and pick her up, spinning her in a twirl. She wraps her arms around my neck, and I lean in to kiss her. Her lips melt into mine, and I break the kiss, smiling.

"Maybe I should teach you things more often." She jokes.

"Apparently, I have a lot to learn with you." I laugh.

SEVENTEEN

Alana

Harmony didn't come over this weekend, and it was the longest three days of my life. She had her daughter, Millie, from Friday night to Monday morning. We texted the whole time she was free, which wasn't very much. But I love how devoted she is to her daughter, giving over all her attention, just like she did with me when we were together. She also said she'll be done working on the house this week, which means I'll be seeing her even less. I clearly am getting very attached.

Harmony shows up at noon and greets me with a kiss in the doorway. I'm backed against the wall, and she kisses me until I'm breathless.

"I missed you," she murmurs against my lips.

"I missed you too." I smile.

"Why don't we go out for a bit?"

"Where?"

"Will you ever let me take you on a date without asking so many questions?" She laughs.

"Probably not," I admit.

"Fair enough. I thought we'd grab lunch in town. I've been meaning to try the seafood place if that's okay with you." She smiles. I give myself a moment to take in Harmony's outfit. High waisted brown pants, with a gold loop belt, a white button-down that's tucked into her pants but completely open, exposing a tan and orange lace bodysuit that shows off her abs and tattoos. Fuck. I want to stand back and just look at her in this outfit.

"That sounds perfect, and I know how to dress for that."

Thankfully, Wrenn and Gemma gathered all my things from Will over the weekend. It's still in a bit of disarray, but I had the perfect dress to wear. I find it and check that it's free from wrinkles. It's a mixed pattern of brown, maroon, and pink, with long sleeves that falls mid-knee. My hair is already styled with smooth waves, and I've repainted my nails. I was tired of looking at my wedding nails, so I painted them a warm red to go with the fall vibes. It's almost October, after all. I pair it with my tall, brown riding boots. But what makes the outfit the best is the lingerie I'm hiding underneath it. I don't know if anything will happen later, but here's to hoping.

"All set." I tuck my phone into my purse and follow Harmony to her car. She holds the door open for me and makes sure my dress is safe before shutting it behind me.

The Salty Waves is a town staple, opening before I was born. My family and I often eat lunch here. It's one of the nicer options in town. And since the water is right there, the seafood is always fresh. I don't mention to Harmony that I'd been here just a few weeks earlier with my friends.

"Everything sounds so good, is it as good as it sounds?" Harmony asks, looking over the menu.

"Oh, yes. I always eat way too much."

"Holy shit, are these cheesy biscuits like at Red Lobster?" Harmony's eyes go wide as the waiter delivers a basket of them.

"Shhh, they don't like being compared to that place." I hush her. "But yes, almost identical."

She takes a bite of one and groans. "Shit, this is good. Sorry, I have a mouth like a sailor, don't I? I should probably clean that up. I'm usually better when I'm used to being around Millie."

"I don't mind it." I smile. Another reminder of how different she is compared Will.

"Can I take your order?" The waiter comes back.

"I'll have the lobster bisque soup in a bread bowl please," I tell him.

"And I'll have the lobster linguine." Harmony and I hand him the menus.

"Anything to drink?"

"Oh, just water for me." Harmony smiles.

"Diet Coke with extra ice?"

"Perfect, I'll be right back with your drinks."

"So, tell me about your daughter," I say.

"Really?"

"Yeah, I mean unless you don't want to. But I feel like I'd love to know more about her. Is that weird?" I start to second guess myself.

"No. Uh, she's almost seven. She is obsessed with everything girly or sparkly or unicorns. She loves swinging at the park and has a bit of beef with her friend because she can go a little higher. She hates bananas but loves spinach. I don't know why. She lives with her mom during the week, unless she's working or something, and then I'll get extra time with her. Oh, and her favorite color is pink."

"She's in the second grade then? Or is that first?" I try to do the math in my head.

"Second, she's one of the younger kids in her class, I think."

"My best friend, Kim, teaches at the elementary school. But she teaches Kindergarten," I say.

"What's her last name?"

"Stewart."

"She's on the PTA with Jamie. They're planning some kind of Halloween dance, I think." Harmony smiles.

"I believe that. Kim likes to help out with what she can. Are you on the PTA?"

"No, I was, but a lot of the moms like to go out for wine. At least the moms in Chicago did. So Jamie started going instead."

"Does that happen a lot? Where things that shouldn't have alcohol, do?" I ask.

She sighs, "Yeah. It's something I think about a lot. Like I can't go to a bar and meet someone, and by someone, I mean a friend. And then so many adult activities are centered around drinking. This wasn't really something I noticed until I got sober, but it's a little annoying. Like, why does it have to be paint and sip? Why can't it just be painting."

"You're right. My friends and I probably went drinking more this summer, doing things that didn't really need it," I admit.

"Like, if I wasn't working on the house for your parents, I never would have met you. We probably wouldn't run in the same circles or go to the same places."

"That's true. My sister is a bartender, so we usually go there to hang out. I mean, I was also supposed to be married by now, so we definitely wouldn't have met in a social setting." I let out an awkward laugh. Who the hell allowed me to be on a date? Wasn't this the type of stuff you were supposed to avoid talking about on dates?

"It's something I wanted to mention, actually. I plan on being sober the rest of my life. Which includes having a sober home. I'm not asking you to decide this now, but it is something I want to put out there. I can't be around alcohol, and I don't want to live my life acting like it doesn't exist, but I definitely don't ever want it in my home. I feel like that should be the one place I can relax without having it. But I understand that's not something everyone wants."

"Okay. I haven't really given it much thought. I mean, I've made a point not to have alcohol in the house since our conversation. But it's not like I've really noticed or missed it. Only once was I going to have a glass, remembered, and had a Diet Coke instead." I laugh.

"I just know it can be a dealbreaker for some. And that's okay. It's a huge life change."

"It's completely valid to want to feel safe in your own home. I'll be sure to give it some thought, but you don't have to worry about me bringing alcohol in the home as long as we're together." I put my hand on top of hers.

"Drinks." The waiter places them in front of us. "Your food should be out shortly."

"Thank you," we both mumble.

"Another thing I should probably bring up, is that Jamie and I have a rule about Millie meeting the people that we date," Harmony starts.

"Okay…"

"We wait until we're serious about someone before she's introduced to anyone. We don't want her getting unnecessarily attached to someone who won't be in her life long-term."

"That makes sense." I hesitate before asking, "Have you both introduced her to many people?"

She chuckles. "I haven't ever introduced her to someone I'm seeing. And Jamie introduced her to someone she was dating once. But that was a while ago and they're no longer together."

I don't hold back my smile. It isn't that I'm jealous she'd dated before me or anything. But I did like hearing that there was no one serious before me, besides her ex-wife. I'm also partly relieved. I love kids, but that doesn't mean I'm ready to meet hers. It sounds intimidating and scary, if you ask me. Kids have no filter and if she didn't like me, there's no telling what would happen between Harmony and me.

The waiter brings us our food, and I audibly groan at how good everything smells. Harmony watches me as I take a big spoonful of my soup and moan. I don't know how there are some people who hate seafood. This was freaking delicious. I can taste the lobster bits in every bite, and I dip in one of the biscuits, making it extra decadent.

"How's yours?" I ask Harmony, looking up from my plate.

"So freaking good." She groans, taking a mouthful of pasta.

"Do you want to try some of mine?" I offer.

"Actually, I really do. Do you want some of mine?"

"Maybe a bite."

Harmony holds out a forkful of pasta for me. I open my mouth, and she puts it in. The sauce drips down my chin slightly, and she catches it with her thumb. She puts her thumb in her mouth, sucking the sauce off while keeping eye contact with me. Fuck. Did it suddenly get really hot in here?

I give Harmony a spoonful of soup and she moans. Like, a full blown, throaty moan. Of course she did, because I barely have any covering. This bodysuit is less panties and more of something to be admired. I clench my thighs together, and Harmony smirks at me. I try to focus on eating, but all my thoughts are now dirty.

"That is really good." She smiles.

I just nod, not trusting my voice right now. We're taking things slow, which I appreciate. Except now I'm freaking horny and the last thing I want is to wait. I'm so curious about being with a woman, and despite my extensive research, nothing will scratch that itch except actually doing it. Specifically with Harmony. As many times as possible. I know I'll like it. If it's with her, I was going to like it. She seemed to know everything I liked.

"You okay? You look a little flushed."

"I'm just hot—it's hot in here," I mumble.

Harmony reaches for my hand. "You're so cute when you're turned on."

I blush even harder. I guess I'm more obvious than I thought.

"I can't help that you're hot." I shrug, acting like I don't care that I was caught.

"Too bad I can't help you with that right now. Maybe later on." She winks.

I almost choke on the spoonful of soup, and she smiles smugly back at me. Did she say what I think she said? Does that mean she wants to hook-up tonight? I'm going to call this my lucky lingerie from now on if that's the case. I won't mention that I bought it for my honeymoon. It wasn't like I'd ever worn it before, and it deserves to get some love and attention. Fuck, *I* deserve to get some love and attention. Harmony's words make me want to sprint through dinner, thinking about the possibility of having her for dessert. But I know it'll be worth the wait.

EIGHTEEN

Harmony

I've been trying to take things slow with Alana but with the way she's looking at me and the sounds she's been making, I'm tempted to take her on this table. Of course, I don't—for a multitude of reasons, mostly being that I don't wish to be arrested for public indecency. But I think Alana's on the same page as me with her hooded eyes and the way she keeps chewing on her bottom lip. We're eating lunch but when she moans during every bite, it was hard not to have a visceral reaction.

"What do you say we take dessert to go and head back to my place?" I ask.

"Uh, yeah, yes. That sounds good." She's nervous but only because she didn't expect me to offer that tonight.

I ask for the dessert menu, ordering the chocolate cake for Alana and the carrot cake for me. We get the check and pay while the dessert is packaged along with our leftovers. Alana's unusually quiet on our drive, so I put my hand on her bare thigh, and she seems to relax.

"You don't have to be nervous. We can do whatever you feel comfortable with," I assure her.

"I'm not nervous, I'm excited." She smiles.

"Maybe I should be nervous then," I joke.

"I'm just happy to get to be with you, in this way."

"I am, too."

When we get to my apartment, I give her a quick tour of the place, stopping at my bedroom last. She excuses herself to the bathroom, and I use the time to get somewhat prepared. I'm not ready in the slightest, so I'm relieved I remembered to make my bed today. I pull everything out of my pockets, like my vape and my phone and anything else I have. I don't want anything falling out when I'm trying to make a move. I grab my box of adult toys from under the bed, locked so Millie doesn't accidentally go scrounging through them. And I put the strap in my nightstand. I don't know what she's up for tonight, but I'd rather not have to ruin the moment looking for it. I also slip a few other things in there too, just in case.

I sit on the bed, trying to be casual when Alana comes back in. She's taken off her boots and dress, standing before me in a black lace bodysuit. It has tiny pink flowers all over it and ruffles on the edges. She stands in the doorway, holding one arm over her head. Her breasts are practically falling out of the thing, and my mouth is watering.

"Holy shit," I mumble. Maybe I'm not ready for this.

"I thought it might ease the tension to surprise you," she whispers.

She saunters toward me, her tan legs on display, her breasts bouncing with every step. I'm about to be a lucky woman. She does a little spin, showing off the back of the outfit, and fuck. Her entire ass is exposed, just ruffles and lace up her back. I glance up her body, all the way back to her smile.

"You wanna do this?" I check.

"Yes. *Please.*"

Closing the distance between us, I reach for her face. I pull her body into mine, holding her cheeks as she looks into my eyes. God, she is so fucking beautiful. She bats her dark eyelashes, and I'm a goner. I press my lips to hers, sliding my tongue in her mouth, and she groans. My hand goes to her neck, gripping it gently. Her hands wrap around my waist, and I feel her reaching for my ass. Taking her by the neck, I push her back onto the bed. She sits, looking up at me with curious eyes.

"I want to worship you, kitten." My hand grips her throat, making her look at me.

She doesn't speak, only nods. I straddle her thighs, kissing her neck. I take the time to nibble on her earlobe the way she likes and blow lightly in her ear. Alana tenses up as I tease her. Her body reacts to each touch. I bite down on her shoulder, giving the smallest amount of pressure. I pull one of the straps of her lingerie down, kissing her collar bone as she pants in anticipation. My hands brushing over the tops of her breasts. Her soft skin fills my hands as I squeeze.

"Mmm," she hums.

"I'm so torn between taking my time with you and fucking you the way I desperately want to," I admit.

"F-fuck me please," she stutters. I smile, not giving away which I'm planning to go.

I slide down the other strap and spring her breasts free. Her pretty pink nipples are hard and alert, begging to be pinched. So I grab one, pinching it with my fingers, and Alana instantly tosses her head back with a throaty moan. Which only makes me do it again, but harder.

"Ohh!" she cries.

I move my hand to the other one, taking the time to tug and tease. Then I dip my head to her chest and pop one into my mouth. I suck and twirl my tongue around her nipple, watching as she struggles to keep her eyes open. She moves her hips under mine, begging for more contact. With my free hand, I steady her struggling hips.

"Have patience, kitten." I don't know where the nickname came from but it's evident, she likes it.

I pull the bodysuit further down her body and she groans. I move my hand between us, and I can feel how wet she is. Her pussy is hot and wet, begging to be touched. So I dip my fingers between the fabric and pop the buttons open with one flick of my wrist.

"Oh!" She squeals. I laugh as I get on my knees.

"I'm going to eat your pussy until you come, okay, kitten?"

"Yes, please." She nods eagerly.

I stare at her pussy, pink like her other lips, dripping for me. A few dark curls over the top is all I see. I can smell her arousal and I've barely gotten started. I take a steady, teasing lick through her pussy. Alana's body almost floats off the bed as she moans. Gripping her hips, I settle her and push my face into her pussy. Without warning, I devour her. Her sweet taste, her juices dripping down my chin and face. She's clenching the bedsheets until she reaches for my hair. Gripping it tightly, she pulls, which only spurs me on. I suck on her clit, taking it in my mouth.

"Holy fuck! Oh, Harmony!" she cries out in pleasure.

I hum against her, making sure there's not an inch of her pussy I haven't tasted. She pulls harder on my hair, and I brush my teeth across her clit. Not enough to hurt, but enough to tease. She screams, begging me not to stop.

"Right there! Holy fuck!" she calls, and I don't stop. I suck harder on her clit, my tongue and jaw working overtime to please her. "Yes!"

She screams, achieving her orgasm, and I smile. Only stopping when she taps the side of my head. I wipe my mouth off casually before reaching to help her take off her body suit completely. I toss it on the ground and then get up to get her some water. I bring her a glass, telling her to drink, and she does.

"I didn't know sex could be like *that*," she admits with a blush.

"Didn't know a woman could come that fast." I wink.

"It's been a while!"

"Not that long since you had a little self-care. I heard you once in the shower." I smirk.

Alana's jaw drops. "You heard me!? How?"

"Maybe make sure the bathroom window is closed next time you want to moan in the shower," I tease.

"Oh, my God! That was WEEKS AGO. Why didn't you tell me?"

"It was hot and also none of my business. It's not like I saw anything. Just heard those sexy moans," I say.

"I'm so embarrassed." She covers her face with her hands, but I reach for them.

"There's nothing to be embarrassed about! Everyone does it." I shrug.

"Now that I wouldn't mind seeing."

Alana reaches for me, and I lean in to kiss her. My hands are on her breasts, playing and squeezing, while she reaches for my belt, undoing it and untucking my shirt from my pants. She slides her hand down my tattooed chest, all the way down to my hip bones. She pulls me closer to her and I groan. I'm not normally one to let a woman take control, but something came over me. I wanted to see where this went.

"Can I fuck you?" she asks, batting her eye lashes like she didn't just ask that.

"Of course, kitten."

She tugs down my pants, tossing them aside, and then pulls off my underwear, which are more boy shorts than panties. I didn't know if this was happening, but I'm not ashamed to say I've been waxed for the last week, just in case. A small landing strip is the only thing down below. I watch Alana's expressions, her desire only building as she sees how wet I am. She's curious in her movements, and I bite on my lip, trying to give her a moment to explore.

Alana dips her fingers in my pussy, touching my lips and then sliding one finger inside just a touch. When I gasp, she looks at me worriedly and pulls it out quickly. I smile, and she tries again, this time sliding her fingers inside a little deeper. I groan, and she moves them in more until she can't anymore. She then moves her thumb to brush over my clit. When I buck my hips into her hand, she smiles. She's having fun and I'm getting teased.

"Please remember I'm all for exploring, but you are teasing me."

"Maybe that's what I want to do." She smirks smugly.

Oh shit. I hadn't even considered that. But then she curls her fingers inside me and starts to pump them in and out. While her thumb touches my clit, she presses kisses on my hip bone. Her free hand reaches for my breasts, still protected by my bra. Every once in a while, I liked to wear something fancier. I usually stick to sports bras most days, but I wanted to look nice.

"How does that feel?" she asks, looking up at me from between my breasts.

"So good." I groan.

Alana moves her fingers expertly and I keep my eyes on her. Dark curls surround my body as her hair gets everywhere. I can see her ass bouncing in the air behind her, and I groan. Her fingers pump in and out as my orgasm builds. I grip the sheets just as Alana scratches her nails down my chest and I moan.

"Fuck yes!" I cry out. Alana keeps going, encouraging me through my orgasm until I lie back, exhausted.

Alana carefully pulls out her fingers. I'm about to offer her a tissue when she holds them up quizzically and pops one in her mouth. Her eyes light up like she likes the taste, and I watch my girl suck her fingers clean. Fuck. That's a fucking image to be saved for later. She curls up next to me and I relax. Her hair tickles my arm, but I'll be damned if I ask her to move it.

"So, that was sex with a woman," she says.

"Any thoughts?"

"How the hell have I never tried this before?" she asks with a laugh.

"Well, any time you'd like to try again, I'm here." I wink. She playfully shoves me, but I grip her wrist, pulling it over her head and climbing on top of her. Her eyes widen as looks at me, waiting to see what might come next.

NINETEEN

Alana

"Have we really been having sex for four hours?!" I exclaim.

Harmony chuckles. "Time flies when you're having fun?"

"I think you've given me more orgasms today than I've ever had in my entire life." I smile.

"Happy to be of help." Harmony winks. She passes me a glass of water, and I take a little sip.

"How the hell do lesbians ever do anything else? It's not like we need to stop coming, we could keep going and going."

"Well, eventually one of us will be tired or at least need some food."

My stomach growls as if on cue. "I could go for some food."

"What are you in the mood for?"

"We never ate our dessert!" I exclaim. "Crap, did we leave it in your car? It's probably smush by now." It's still hot for an October day.

"Don't worry, I put it in the fridge when we came in," she assures me. "I'll be right back."

"Okay, I'm going to pee."

Harmony gets out of bed, walking naked to the kitchen. Which is a sight to admire. Her back tattoos are on display and her tight ass is even firmer without those pants on. Fuck. I pick up her button-down shirt, slipping it on, and head to the bathroom. When I glance at my hair, I realize what a mess it is. I try to tame it, but it's no use, so I tie it in a messy bun with a rubber band I find in her cabinet. When I head back to the room, Harmony has the pillows propped up and is holding our dessert out in front of her.

"I know I got the carrot cake, but I might have to steal a piece of that chocolate cake, it looks to die for," she says.

"Only if you eat it off me."

"I don't know if that's the challenge you think it is." She laughs.

I climb into bed with her, she takes a little scoop of chocolate frosting and wipes it on my collar bone. It's cold but refreshing. She leans in, licking it off and sucking my collarbone clean.

"Shit, that was hotter than I anticipated," I mumble.

"Come get sustenance, I don't want you passing out on me," she orders.

I take a fork from her and eat some of the cake. "Holy crap, this is so good."

"Next time, I definitely get the chocolate cake." She laughs.

"I know we're still getting to know each other sexually but are there any things you like a lot or absolutely hate doing in bed," Harmony asks, taking a bite of her cake.

"Is this where you tell me you're into feet or peeing on people?" I tease.

"Hey! Don't kink shame, this is a safe space." She laughs. "But no, that's not my thing."

"Honestly, I've only been with men who liked missionary and didn't know where the clit was."

"That is so sad." Harmony frowns.

"Like, I don't even know what I like because I've never had someone to explore with. Are there things you like?"

"Yeah, I love taking a woman with a strap. Switching positions and having her beg me to come. There's something about being in control."

"I picked up on that." I blush. "I don't think I'd like being in control of the strap, but watching you take me with it? I could get behind that."

"I think you mean in front of." Harmony winks.

"Oh, my God!" I toss a pillow at her. Thankfully she grabs it before it goes in the remains of our cake.

"Why don't I clean this up?" Harmony grabs the cake containers and heads to the kitchen.

When she comes back, she stops to check her phone. "I'm sorry, I hate being on my phone when I'm with someone, but I have to check it for Millie. She doesn't have a phone yet, but Jamie texts me updates or Millie will text me from it sometimes."

"It's okay. I think it's nice you communicate with her even on the days you don't have her. I'm sure she appreciates that." I smile.

"I hope so. I try to make it as easy on her as possible." Harmony puts the phone down and crawls back into bed.

Somehow, even though we've been doing this for hours and I've come more times than I can count, I'm still ready to go again. So when she tugs her shirt off of me, I'm ready for whatever's coming next.

"You feel okay?" she asks, checking in.

"Perfect." I smile. Then I lean down and begin kissing her again. My body straddles hers as I grind my hips on her waist.

"I want to savor my time with you," I whisper.

Slipping my body between her legs, I take my time kissing her inner thighs. Sucking lightly on her hips and kissing her pubic bone until I can feel her wiggling under me. She's desperate for me to touch her, and fuck if I'm not, too. I've never done this before, so I'm a little bit nervous and hesitant. What if I do something she hates and she's so turned off we have to stop? What if she doesn't like me going down on her because I'm bad at it? I try to talk myself out of it. Harmony isn't the type to push me off the bed and tell me I suck, that much I knew. She'll talk me through it if I need help.

So I slide my tongue between her thighs and taste her for the first time all day. Tasting her is like finding a new favorite food. I only want to taste her and her alone from now on. She is sweet and in this moment, she's all mine. She starts bucking her hips to my face and I look up at her, from her core.

"Oh, God. You look so good between my legs, kitten." She moans. Her breath is heavy, and I lick long and slow, trying to sop up every last drop of her.

I move my hands to her chest, taking her nipples between my fingers and pulling. Just enough to feel her getting wetter from my touch. So much so that I slide my hand down, cupping it around her sex, and press hard. Harmony screams at my touch, and I smile. There's nothing more satisfying than pleasuring a woman like this. I want to watch her body react like this again and again. It's nothing like going down on a man. Harmony's body is soft and delicate. Her pussy is delicious and only made me want to keep going. This was as much of a turn on for me as it was for her. My wetness was already sliding down my thighs.

Going back between her thighs, I try to remember what she did to me. But honestly, it's all pleasure and feeling. So I go based on her, paying close attention to her moans and gasps. The way her body moves under my touch. I take long, soft licks down her pussy. From her clit to below, watching the way she lights up as I get her closer to coming.

"Fuck, kitten. I love the way you do that." She groans. Her hand tangles in my hair and I relax.

One hand is on her breast, playing with her nipple, and the other one I use to press down on her pelvic bone. I suck gently on her clit, and her breathing shifts.

"Holy fuck, please don't stop." She moans. Her breath gets heavier, and she pants more as she gets closer.

I look up at her, watching her face as she comes undone. I've never seen her more relaxed. Her body convulsing and her face peaceful. She orgasms, her mouth forming a perfect O as she moans. I stop when she stops moving, wiping off my face and sliding next to her in bed.

"Was that okay?" I ask anxiously. I'm not normally one to need praise but, I do want to be good at everything.

"How can you even ask that? I just fucking came on your face." Harmony laughs. "It was so fucking good."

She pulls me in for a kiss, and I melt. Our naked bodies become an array of naked limbs. Her legs tangle with mine as our bodies press against the other. We kiss just a few times before relaxing into the pillows behind us. Harmony pulls the blankets over us, and I feel my eyes beginning to flutter shut. I don't even know what time it is, but I feel exhausted.

Harmony starts to rub my arm, her thumb tracing small circles along the side. I yawn and she smiles at me. We're both so quiet in this moment. But the way she's looking at me makes me feel like I'm floating. Her eyes follow my gaze, looking over my body and then back at me. She looks so relaxed, like someone falling asleep for the first time. I don't know if there's anything more to say.

I've never felt like this before. The way butterflies flutter in my chest. The safeness I feel wrapped in her arms. There's no stress here, only a cloud like aura of thoughts. I wish I had a better way to describe it. I just know this was never how I felt with Will. Not that we often laid like this, not unless I begged him to. It always felt awkward and weird. Like our bodies didn't belong together. He was always thinking about something else, never truly being here with me. But looking at Harmony, I can tell she is nowhere but here, feeling this moment with me.

Her fingers glide across my skin like melted butter on a hot pan. I move her blue curls out of her eyes, brushing my hand down her cheek and across her sharp jaw. She smiles under my touch. Her blue eyes light up as I snuggle up closer to her. I feel scared by how good this feels. The nerves slowly creep up, so I do my best to push them down. I don't need to worry about that right now. I can stress about it and what this all means later. Right now, I just want to enjoy this moment and how good it feels being with her.

TWENTY

Harmony

Alana and I somehow manage to spend the next several days in bed. Switching between my bed at my apartment and Alana's bed at the estate house, as she calls it. We spend most of the time naked, except for the two days I spend finishing the last of the projects and cleaning up. Her parents are happy with the end result, which leads to a bonus deposit into my account. I'm not sure if they know I'm sleeping with their daughter or how happy they'd be then, but for now, I'm happy.

The only thing that's bothering me was the fact that we haven't really had *the talk* yet. Alana seems to be all in with me, but she's also the same woman I saw fleeing the hotel just a month ago. Were we moving too fast for someone who just got out of a relationship? I don't know how she feels because any time I attempt to bring it up, she somehow distracts me. Usually with her tongue on my belly button. But whatever it was, I was distracted. I don't know if she's avoiding the conversation on purpose but, when I wake up alone today, I decide it's time to talk.

"Hello!" Alana smiles as I walk into her place.

"Hey." I kiss her lips and follow her inside.

"I didn't know what time you were coming, but my sister brought muffins over. She's in the kitchen and sort of wants to meet you. I tried to text and warn you, but she stole my phone." She grimaces.

"Your sister is here?"

"Yeah, Wrenn. Even though I'm the big sister, she kind of has always been protective of me. But especially now, so she wanted to meet you. She's leaving with her girlfriend next week for their trip," she explains.

"Okay." I nod.

I wasn't expecting this, but I also didn't mind. It isn't like there's family for Alana to meet, but I liked the idea of meeting Alana's family. Sure, I already know her parents, but they don't seem the most pleasant or the most open to meeting someone their daughter is dating or sleeping with. At least Wrenn would probably be up front with me about how she feels.

I turn the corner and find her sister sipping an iced coffee. She's shorter than Alana and me, with dark purple hair and a ton of piercings. She has tattoos all over her body and is dressed in all black. If I had seen her on the street, I'd have no idea this was Alana's little sister.

"Hey, I'm Harmony. Alana said you wanted to meet me?"

Wrenn stands, shaking my hand and sizing me up. "I was curious who the woman was that got my sister on the dark side."

"You know what they say, we do have cookies." I didn't know how the joke would land, but Wrenn cracks a smile.

"She says you have a kid?"

"Oh yeah, she's almost seven. Light of my life." I smile.

"So you've been married before?" She raises an eyebrow.

"I have. We're on good terms."

"Good terms, like Alana should be worried you're still in love with your ex-wife?"

"Wrenn!" Alana scolds her sister.

I crack a smile. She reminds me of a sitcom dad who sits on

the couch sipping a beer and cleaning his gun while the daughter's boyfriend sits there nervously. Charlie Swan immediately comes to mind.

"Not at all. Good terms like, we don't fight in the parking lot of my daughter's school, but we also never want to be married again." I laugh.

"I'm so sorry. Wrenn, you don't need to ask such personal questions." Alana rolls her eyes at Wrenn.

"I'm just looking out for you. What are your intentions with her?"

"Wrenn!" she yells again, then turns to me. "I swear you don't have to answer this."

"I was hoping she'd be my girlfriend, but it isn't a conversation I've broached with Alana yet. I don't ask that lightly and I like to know I'm on the same page with someone," I explain. I can feel Alana's eyes on me, but I don't look her way.

"I like her." Wrenn smiles after a moment. "You should snatch her up before one of our friends does."

"Oh, my God, don't you have somewhere to be?" Alana starts pushing Wrenn out the door, almost spilling her iced coffee.

"Let me know if you ever need dirt on this one! I can tell you TONS of stories!" Wrenn calls out as Alana shoves her out the front door.

"I am so sorry for that." Alana shakes her head, but I'm laughing.

"It was very entertaining. And I like how much she cares about you." I smile.

"We weren't always close, but in the last few years we've really been there for each other. I don't know what I'm going to do while she's away."

"I guess you'll have to put up with me."

"Did you really mean what you said? About me being your girlfriend?" she asks quietly.

"Yeah, I was actually coming over here to talk about that. I know we've kind of avoided it until now, but I'd like to make it official."

"What does that mean exactly?"

"Well, you'd be my girlfriend, and we'd only see each other."

"I like the idea of it."

"But?"

"I just don't know if I'm ready. I know how good I feel when I'm with you. And I don't just mean the sex, I mean it makes me happy just being around you. But I was just engaged to someone else less than six weeks ago. I don't know if I'm supposed to be taking more time or something. There's no guide for how to navigate this." She sighs.

I take her hand in mine and look at her. "There isn't a rule book, it's only a matter of what you feel ready for. But if you aren't ready to commit, that's okay. I can wait until you are ready. As long as you think it will eventually head that direction."

"I do think it will, just not yet." She nods.

"I understand." I am a little bit disappointed but not surprised. I knew this might be the case when I asked.

"But I'm not seeing anyone else. I only want to see you. I just am not ready to call this serious yet," she clarifies. Somehow that makes me feel a little bit better.

"That's okay," I reassure her. I don't love it, but I know where she's coming from.

"Can I ask you something about drinking?" Alana asks softly.

"Of course, what's going on?"

"I know you go to meetings, usually once a week or more. But do you have a sponsor? And how does that work?"

I relax. These are easy questions to answer. "I do, her name is Ruby. I met her while I still lived in Chicago. She's about twenty years older than me and sort of like the mother figure I don't have. I call her when I need to. Sometimes we chat just for fun because she's sort of like family to me. Millie knew her as Aunt Ruby." I smile.

"Do you sponsor anyone?"

"No, I don't think I'm ready for that yet. I do have years under my belt but personally also having Millie and work, I don't have the time to dedicate to someone else right now," I explain.

"That makes sense. And does a sponsor just give advice or is she more like a therapist?"

"It depends on the sponsor. Ruby will kick my ass if I need it. She's not afraid to tell me I'm wrong or that I shouldn't be doing something. She knows what my priorities are in life so if she sees me swaying, she'll remind me. But for the most part we just talk about life. I'm friends with several of the other people she sponsors too. We all used to joke we were her children."

"And your drinking—I want to be sensitive here—but was it, like, bad?"

"Yes." I sigh. "I was drinking almost twenty-four seven, and I was a wreck because of it," I admit.

"I see."

"I'm not telling you this to scare you, I just feel if you're going to be in whatever this is with me, you should know the truth. I'm in recovery now but it's not like I'll ever be able to have a drink again. I've made peace with that but it's a battle every day to stay that way," I explain.

"I think you're really strong. I just wanted to know what it was like for you. I don't need to know any details, but I think for now at least, I'd be happy to be sober with you. I'd rather have you in my life than alcohol."

"Really?" My eyes tear up a little. It means more to me than I can explain.

"Yeah." I pull her in for a kiss. "Why don't we go celebrate this?"

"Oh, yeah?" She catches my vibe and races me to her bedroom.

We're both racing to pull off our clothes faster than the other and climb into bed. I pull Alana on top of me, and she grinds her body on mine. She bends down to kiss me, and I feel her lips as her tongue slips in my mouth. She sucks lightly on my bottom lip, causing me to groan into her mouth. Fuck. I run my hands down her back, gripping her ass with two hands. Full and plenty, pushing her hips into mine. Alana starts kissing my neck, sucking a little too hard when I pull her back by the throat to stop her.

"No hickies, I can't have my daughter asking why I have a bruise on my neck." I laugh.

"No visible ones, then?" Her eyebrows raise.

"Fuck, kitten. Yes, no visible ones." She dips her head to my chest, sucking on the sides of my breast until I'm moaning. She only stops when she pulls back to see her work. She repeats this over and over, until my chest is covered in them.

Alana takes control today, putting herself between my thighs. I usually love taking control but there is something exhilarating about seeing her there. Her dark eyes stare at me through hooded eyelids. Her dark eyelashes bat away as her tongue dances on my clit. I'm already wet, her body making me like a horny teenager.

"God, you're so wet already. Is that all for me?" She smirks as she drags two fingers through my folds.

"Yes." I groan. She was teasing me. "Please don't tease."

"Don't tell me what to do." She pouts.

"Sorry, kitten." I laugh. She's so fucking cute.

Alana positions herself between my legs, kissing my inner thighs and trailing the lines of one of my tattoos. She hums softly against my pussy like a kitten in heat. I love the way she gets so into it. It's hard to believe I'm the first woman she's ever been with. Alana slides two fingers inside me, twirling them around before finding my G-spot.

"Oh!" I cry out. I hate being teased, but once she really starts, it will only take minutes to finish.

"That's it." She coaches.

Her fingers curl, pumping in and out while her mouth latches onto my clit. I gasp, moaning her name softly, and she looks up at me with satisfied eyes. I'm useless under her touch. I move my hips, creating friction with her tongue. She moves faster and I chase the orgasm. Heat builds in my lower stomach as my legs begin to shake.

"Holy fucking shit!" I cry out as I come. It takes a few minutes for me to come down from my orgasm, but when I do, Alana is lying next to me, smiling.

"You're hot when you come," she says softly. "I want to do it again."

"Okay, what are you thinking?"

"I want you to sit on my face..." She trails her fingers down my chest and my eyes widen. I'm not usually the one to sit on someone's face. Women usually sit on my face.

"Are you sure?"

"I'm very sure." Alana nods and lays down on her bed, setting up the pillows so we'll both be comfortable.

I'm hesitant until I think about how good it will feel to have Alana's tongue on me again. I shake off all my thoughts, hold on to the headboard, and climb over her. I position myself over her face, kneeling on the bed with my pussy just above her mouth. I look down at her expectant face and shiver. She smiles and I lower myself slowly, careful not to put all my weight on her. But she pulls me down, almost causing me to lose my balance. Her tongue connects with my pussy, and I gasp out loud. She brushes slow strokes over my slit and begins sucking slowly on my clit. I grip the headboard to steady myself and call out a multitude of curses I can't hold back.

"Fuck, that feels so good, kitten." I begin moving my hips to get her to go faster.

She picks up the pace, sucking on my clit while I reach backward and grab her breasts. I take her nipple between my fingers, and she moans into my pussy. I tug tightly on her nipples, and I rock my hips as she moves her tongue.

"Don't fucking stop, kitten." I groan.

She goes even faster this time, and I ride her face until my hip starts to hurt a little bit. It's a bit of a weird position, but I don't want to stop. She feels so freaking good. And looking down to see Alana between my thighs is something out of a wet dream. Like, holy shit. I rock my hips forward on her lips, letting her tongue twirl around inside me, and that's when I feel it.

Holy fucking shit.

"Yes! Don't stop, kitten!" I cry out. I grip the headboard, and she doesn't let up.

It's not until I'm seeing stars that I roll over off her and onto the pillows. I'm breathless and this time, it's Alana who brings me a glass of water. She perches herself on my chest like a kitten, and I groan. I'm seriously falling for this woman.

TWENTY-ONE

Alana

I went back to work last week, and it went better than I anticipated. There were a few new client folders sitting on my desk, and instead of choosing the ones that brought home the biggest bottom line, I took on the ones that brought the most joy. I mostly work from home, occasionally going to the office, usually just to make sure no one needs anything from me and I'm up to date on my mail. The clients I took on make me excited to choose things for them, furniture and wallpaper and everything in-between. They're creating a home with as much color as possible. They are two artists looking for a home that brings them creative joy.

Harmony has Millie for the weekend at her house, so I'm working on my laptop in the backyard. It's a bit chilly, so I'm huddled under a soft blanket while I look at the colors of the changing leaves. I wish I could see her this weekend, but at least I got to see her last night. We had another sleepover until she had to go to work. I appreciate how much time she made for me when she's working and has Millie. I try not to bother her when she has her, knowing how much she enjoys her time with Millie. I don't want to intrude on Millie's time with her mother either. Which is why I'm surprised when Harmony calls me.

"Hello?" I say into the phone.

"Thank goodness, hi. I'm freaking out a bit and I don't know what to do." Harmony sounds stressed and panicked on the other end.

"Okay, what's going on? Are you okay?" I ask, trying not to overreact.

"A pipe burst at my apartment and everything is flooded. I called the landlord, and he didn't pick up, so I called a plumber and he's out of town because it's Columbus Day weekend. Which I told him doesn't exist, it's Indigenous People's Day, but then he hung up on me. So I called the second plumber in town and he's also out of town so I don't know what to do. He said he can be here tomorrow night, but I can't stay here with Millie. There's water everywhere. I'm not a plumber and I don't know what the hell to do," Harmony says, somehow in one long breath.

"Okay. Why don't you bring her here?" I suggest.

"What? Like you want to watch her? Alana I—"

"No no! I meant why don't you bring her here and you both stay? We have like, four or five bedrooms. You two can stay in one or you both get your own. Either way."

"I don't know…"

"I can even hide out in my room if you need or see if I can spend the night at someone else's house. It just doesn't make sense not to come here if you have nowhere else to go," I explain.

"I thought about calling Jamie but she's out of town and I know she doesn't have a spare key anywhere. Maybe we could just spend the night at a hotel or something…" She sighs.

"I'm serious Har, I don't want you to spend unnecessary amounts of money on a hotel on top of paying for a plumber. I'll call my sister right now and see if I can stay the night with her. I can leave you a key and everything," I insist.

"I don't want to put you out. But it's a big step, having Millie meet you."

"You don't have to introduce me as your girlfriend or anything. I can be just a friend. I just don't want you stressed about where to sleep. I'd love to meet her if that was okay with you."

"Are you sure?"

"I wouldn't lie to you. I'm happy to make whatever work. I know it's only temporary."

Harmony pauses. It's so quiet on the phone that I almost think she hung up. But then she hums like she's thinking about it. I know she and I had talked about me not meeting Millie until we're serious, but it seems like extenuating circumstances. I know I'm not ready to be alone with Millie, and I'm sure I'm not on her ex-wife's approved babysitter's list. But I also don't want Harmony spending money she probably doesn't have.

"Okay. I'm going to give Jamie a call, so she knows what's going on. And I'm trying to soak up as much as I can. Salvage what I can and move things here. So we'll be there in like, an hour or two. Is that okay?" Harmony sighs.

"Of course."

"Thank you, Alana," she says softly.

"Don't worry about it."

When we hang up, I jump up to clean up the place. It isn't dirty, but I want to make sure the place is child proofed. She's six, so it isn't like I need to make sure she won't eat dirt off the floor, but I move anything adult to my room. And hide the sex toys in my closet. Just in case. I grab sheets from the closet for the other bedrooms. I have a feeling Harmony will want to stay with Millie in one room, so I pick the room with the queen-sized mattress. I change the sheets and open the window a smidge to get some fresh air circulating.

I toss all the old sheets and my laundry in the washing machine. I might as well do a load to get some stuff done while I have time. Then I check the fridge for some food. I don't know what Millie likes, but I have enough ingredients that we could make something. Or maybe we'll just order pizza. I mean, every kid likes pizza, don't they?

I'm tossing everything into the dryer when my phone buzzes with a text telling me they're here. All of a sudden, I'm full of nerves. What if Millie doesn't like me? What if she figures out we are dating and decides she hates me? I'm more nervous than when I had to meet Will's parents. It is definitely more intimidating. can kids smell fear like dogs?

"Hi." I smile, opening the door.

"Alana, this is my daughter Millie. Millie, say hi and thank you to Alana." Harmony instructs.

Behind her appears a taller than I anticipated child with long dark curls and bright blue eyes. She's wearing a T-shirt that says, *I axolotl questions* with a picture of a pink axolotl on it, and a purple, glittery skirt.

"Hi! I'm Millie, thank you Alana. Mama says you guys are new friends. We had a LOT of water in her house. I thought my stuffies were going to drown. Mama let me bring them in the car with us, but she said I could only bring two inside." Millie walks in and talks a mile a minute.

"It's nice to meet you. Come on in, I love your skirt."

"Thank you! My mommy got it for me, not this one but my other one. Some people get confused because they only have one mom and one dad. Do you have two moms or two dads or one of each? My other mom, Mommy, is away for the weekend. I think she went to New York. Have you been to New York? I haven't."

"Mills, give Alana a second to answer," Harmony says with a laugh. "Sorry."

"It's cool, I have one mom and one dad. And I have been to New York but only once when I was in college. It's nice but a lot of walking and the people aren't as friendly as they are here," I tell her.

"I see." She contemplates my answers.

"I didn't know where you'd want to sleep, so I set up one bedroom with the biggest bed and two other bedrooms. I'll show you and you can leave your things there," I tell them. They follow me down the hallway with their bags.

"Mama, can you stay with me?" Millie asks looking up at Harmony.

"Of course." She nods. "We'll stay in here."

They plop their bags on the floor next to the dresser and Millie puts her stuffed bunny and unicorn on the bed.

"Do they have names?" I ask.

"Yes! I got Bunny when I was only three, so I named her Bunny. But I got my unicorn when I was older and her name is Princess Sparkles," she says as if three was eons ago and she's decades older now.

"I love it. I used to have a cat stuffie named Glitter Pants, but that was a long time ago," I tell her.

"Why don't you play on your tablet in here for a little bit? I need to talk to Alana about something in the kitchen," Harmony says.

"That's code for grown up talk." Millie makes a face but grabs her tablet out of her bag and hops on the bed. She looks like a queen sitting in the middle of it.

I follow Harmony to the kitchen, and she loses the fake smile she was holding onto for Millie. She sighs and her shoulders slump in exhaustion. I want to reach out and hug her, but I'm not sure what to do since Millie's here.

"Thank you for letting us stay. I'm sorry it was so last minute and everything. I don't think Jamie is going to be thrilled about you and Millie meeting without me even mentioning I'm seeing someone. But I hope she'll understand the circumstances." She sighs.

"I would think so, and we're not telling her who I am anyway. Give her a chance to warm up to me first."

"She already likes you, I can tell. I mean, I knew she would.

But it's also a relief." Harmony reaches for my hand and intertwines my fingers with hers.

"I hoped she would."

"I can take care of everything this weekend. Food and cooking and such. Like, I don't know what you were up to but please don't feel like you have to entertain us."

"I was working a little on my laptop earlier, but I don't have any pressing work. I thought maybe we'd keep it simple and order a pizza tonight? If you wanna put on a movie or something, that's cool. I'd like to hang out with you both since you're here. But if you'd like me to give you space, that's okay too," I say.

"You want to hang out with us?" Harmony smiles at me, surprised.

"Duh, I'd love to get to know Millie. I know it's sooner than we planned but if it's okay with you, I'd like to be around. I can also go to my sister's tomorrow and give you guys some mama and me time. I was supposed to go help her pack things up for storage before her trip," I explain.

"Yeah, I think that sounds perfect. I'll call for the pizza and then we can see what movie Millie wants to watch." Harmony glances around the corner down the hallway before kissing me. It's quick, a lingering peck before she pulls away. It's more of a tease, but I don't complain. I'm just happy that she's here.

Harmony leaves to call the pizza place and grab Millie. I grab the remote for the TV and pick a spot on the couch to sit while I wait. Millie and Harmony come out a few minutes later, Millie racing for the other couch.

"Mama said we could watch Encanto! It's one of my FAVORITE movies!" Millie jumps up and down.

"I actually don't know that one, do you know which app it's on?" I ask.

"Disney+, I can type it in the search thing if you want. I learned how to spell it," she says proudly.

"You got it." I hand her the remote and watch as she spells the movie. It pops up for her.

As she cheers, Harmony sits on the couch with me. At the other end, with none of us touching. Millie is bouncing up and down, so I can see why she picked sitting with me. I just wish I could reach out and hold her hand.

TWENTY-TWO

Harmony

The closing credits to *Encanto* come on, and Millie is looking at me with puppy dog eyes, asking if she can stay up.

"To do what? It's late." I ask.

"We can dance, it might get the energy out and it's fun." Alana offers.

"Yes! Mama, please?" She clutches her hands together and begs.

"Okay fine." I roll my eyes. If these two ever teamed up against me, I'd be doomed.

"I can play the *Encanto* songs through my record player if I hook up my phone," Alana tells us, and Millie happily agrees.

Alana is setting up the record player when Millie starts looking at the bookshelves next to the TV. It's mostly books and some family photos, so I'm not sure why the interest, but Millie looks puzzled.

"Don't we know her?" Millie points to a photo of Alana's parents and frowns.

"My parents?" Alana looks as confused as I feel.

"YOUR MOM IS THE LADY WHOSE DAUGHTER IS A RUNAWAY BRIDE?!" Millie gasps and the house goes silent. Of course, that's where Millie knew her from. The day of Alana's wedding, we saw all the drama unfold from behind the scenes and I never connected it.

"Uh, what?" Alana looks at me for help.

Millie cuts in first. "We were at the hotel because Mama was putting in new windows. It was super boring, so I was dancing UNTIL I heard people arguing in the hallway. This lady was looking for her daughter. She was supposed to get married and everyone couldn't find her. Was that you?"

"Millie—" I start to say but Alana cuts me off.

"It was."

"You ran away from your own wedding? Why?" Millie looks at her with curious eyes.

"Millie you can't just—"

Alana cuts me off again. "I didn't want to marry someone. I thought I did, but I changed my mind, so I left." She says it simply, and the answer seems to satisfy Millie. I'm impressed with Alana's answer. She wasn't wrong, she didn't lie, and she provided an age-appropriate answer.

Millie switches gears and they start dancing. The music plays until Millie is starting to slow down. Alana seems to catch on, so she winks at me and is the first to say how tired she is. Millie quickly agrees but is happy not to be the first one to admit it. We say goodnight to Alana and head toward our bedroom.

"I like Alana." Millie says as we're brushing our teeth together.

I tread lightly. "You do?"

"Yeah. She likes the same stuff we do, and she's really nice. She's cool." Millie smiles, having no idea that she just gave my girlfriend the biggest seal of approval.

I kiss Millie goodnight, turning off all the lights and tucking her in. She curls up in a ball with her two stuffies. I pick up my phone, scrolling social media for a bit before sending Alana a quick goodnight text. I can't wait to tell her about what Millie said. I'm sure she's worried about it, despite how cool she seemed. Once I'm sure Millie is asleep, I plug my phone in and let myself get some sleep too. I still haven't gotten any confirmation from my landlord or the plumber about the leak, so it seems like we'll be here at least another night.

In the morning, Millie wakes up first. It's just after eight AM, so I remind her to be quiet as we tiptoe to the kitchen. So when I find Alana standing in the kitchen pulling cinnamon buns out of the oven, I'm flabbergasted.

"Good morning," she says in a melodic voice.

"You're up early" I note.

"I was hungry and thought you guys might like some breakfast." She shrugs.

"I love cinnamon buns!" Mille exclaims.

"Me too!" Alana smiles. "I'm going to see my sister today, so you'll have the place to yourselves. Just leave me a key if you decide to go anywhere."

"We're staying here today I think, right Mills?" I look at Millie, who's shoving a cinnamon bun in her mouth.

She mumbles something with her mouth full and I nod. Alana looks at me, confused, and I laugh. "She said yes."

"I did not get that at all." She laughs.

"Mom powers, I can always understand her." I shrug.

Alana has breakfast with us and then gets ready to go. Millie's on her second cinnamon bun when Alana heads out for the day.

"What did you wanna do today?"

"Do you think we could play a board game?" Millie smiles.

"Yeah, I think I brought the Sorry! It's in the car."

"Yay! I wanna be the red!" Millie calls out.

I head to the car to grab the box from my trunk. I saved it from the water along with all my records. Thankfully, I had downsized before we moved here. And thank goodness I still had a stack of boxes, or I'd have nowhere to put any of this stuff.

Millie and I play Sorry! until she wins, and then we play it again until lunch. I make her favorite Mac and cheese while she colors in one of the books she brought. We sit at the table and talk about her week at school.

"I got a one hundred on my spelling test, Mama," she says proudly.

"That's awesome!" I smile.

"I like the school here."

"Better than your old one?"

"Well, the people are nicer here and there's more friends who like the same things I do. But my old one had a better playground. And it depends on the snack, because sometimes it's good and sometimes it's not." I see she's given this a lot of thought.

"Well, Mommy said you're going back to Chicago for Thanksgiving, so you can always see your old friends then."

"Are you coming with us?" Millie perks up.

"No, you'll be visiting Grandma and Grandpa. It's a trip for just you and Mommy," I explain.

"Okay." Millie sighs. "But Grandma always pinches my cheeks so hard."

"I know, but that's because she loves you. You can always put lotion on your cheeks in the car so they're too slippery to pinch."

"That's a great idea!" she exclaims.

Jamie might kill me, but I know how her mother is. Never my biggest fan and loved to pinch cheeks. I don't blame Millie for wanting to protect herself.

"Do you think we can eat outside?" Millie asks.

"Sure, let's get a bowl and our jackets. It's a little chilly today."

"Okay, Mama."

I help her put on her coat, and once we eat our Mac and cheese, Millie is racing around the yard. I have a feeling that was her plan from the start. She loves being outside. She's dancing around, singing some song I've never heard before.

"Hey, Mama, do you think you'll have a birthday party this year?" she asks.

"No, probably not, love."

"That's not fun. How come adults don't have birthday parties?" She frowns.

"That's a good question, I don't really know. I guess because they're mostly for kids? I mean, what would you want me to have one for?"

"I don't know, I just think they're fun." She shrugs.

"We'll have a cake and sing, and maybe Aunt Ruby will come by for the weekend or something," I suggest. She had brought up visiting and I know Millie misses seeing her.

"I'd love that! I love Aunt Ruby!" She jumps up and down.

"My birthday is in two weeks, if she can't come by for it then, we can always plan another trip. Either way, we will definitely be having delicious birthday cake." I smile. I'm a sucker for a good piece of cake.

"Can Mommy come?"

"If Mommy wants to, of course she can." I smile.

I don't know how it would be introducing Alana to my ex-wife on my birthday, but maybe it won't come to that. Somehow, I went from doing nothing to maybe having people over with a cake. I pull out my phone to look at the calendar. My birthday was on a Monday so we would have to celebrate over the weekend or see if Jamie would let me have her that night. I'm sure it wouldn't be a problem since we've switched for birthdays before. I make a mental note to bring it up when I drop off Millie tomorrow.

The next day, I'm pulling into Jamie's driveway and she's standing in the doorway. I can't read her expression because of the sun glaring. Millie runs into her arms and almost knocks Jamie down with the force. They hold each other tightly and I smile at the sight. I know it was hard on Jamie to leave Millie with me, because I felt the same way when she was with Jamie. Millie's telling her all about the weekend when I catch up to them in the house. I want to give Jamie a heads up about a few things before I take off.

"...and we had pancakes for dinner! For dinner, Mommy, isn't that silly? I had so much fun. Mama said we might go back next week if the water isn't fixed." Millie is in the middle of a rambling when I come in.

"Why don't you go get changed into pajamas and we'll talk more soon?" Jamie tells Mille.

"Okay Mommy." She hops down the hallway happily.

"So, what happened this weekend?" Jamie crosses her arms, raising her eyebrow at me.

"A pipe burst in my apartment, and I tried calling a plumber, but no one was around. They're fixing it now, but the damage is so bad that I don't know how long it will take to fix," I explain.

"So where did you stay? She mentioned someone named Alana, is that like a friend or something?"

"I've been working on a client's house for the last month, and I started seeing their daughter."

"So you took her to meet *and* stay with your girlfriend you've had for five whole minutes, and you didn't think to mention it to me?" Jamie keeps her voice low and steady, but I knew she's pissed.

"I introduced Alana to her as a friend. Alana has a place with five bedrooms and knew it would be a waste of money to stay at a hotel., so she let us crash there this weekend. I never left them alone and Millie only knows we're friends. It's still new, so I hadn't told you about it yet, but it was one of my only options this weekend," I explain.

"Oh. That makes sense then. You stayed in the same bedroom as Millie?" she asks. I knew what she was really asking, *did I stay in the same room as my girlfriend with Millie there?*

"Yes. We shared a queen-sized bed the whole night and I locked the door. I know how to keep my daughter safe. But I also wouldn't be dating anyone that I thought would want to bring our daughter harm."

"I know you wouldn't. I'm just a little thrown off guard. We promised we'd talk about this kind of thing first." She sighs.

"I know. And if it wasn't extenuating circumstances then I promise I would have," I agree.

Jamie sighs. She knows me well enough to know if she had been around, I would've just brought her home. "Are you serious about this girl?"

Not missing a beat, I reply, "I am."

"I haven't known you to want to introduce anyone to Millie since our divorce, so this woman must be pretty special." She smiles.

"She is. I'm giving it more time before Millie officially knows who she is, but I'd like them to get to know each other if that's okay with you."

"That's okay with me. You know our agreement. I just don't want Millie getting attached to anyone who might not stick around."

"I know. I don't want that either."

TWENTY-THREE

Alana

Millie and Harmony are only gone a few hours and I already start to miss them. I had so much fun this weekend and I wasn't expecting to feel so attached to them already. Millie was incredibly smart and clearly had Harmony's charisma. She was utterly charming and so much fun to be around. I always knew I wanted to be a mom and have kids someday, but I had never thought of it in this way. I don't think I'd mind having Millie around all the time. She makes me fall harder for Harmony. Like I'm falling for a second part of her. Maybe one day we'd have kids of our own, or maybe Millie would be enough for the two of us.

As I clean up the bedroom they stayed in, I think about what it would be like to have them here all the time. I mean not twenty-four-seven, but as much as Harmony had Millie. Not that I was going to live here forever. This was a temporary stepping stone until I could find my own place and move out. I wasn't suddenly going to move in with Harmony after not being able to commit to being her girlfriend, but maybe somewhere down the line.

Harmony made me feel safe and confident in a way that I've never felt with another person before. She allows me to be authentically myself while giving me the room to grow as a person. Harmony and I connected and appreciated being together without feeling like I was being smothered or being too much to her. She held my hand in public and wanted to spend all of her time with me. Which made me want to spend my time with her too. I loved how I felt when I was around her.

I put the sheets in the laundry when I hear a knock at the door.

"Hey, I know I was just here but I dropped Millie off with Jamie and I wanted to see you. I hope that's okay." Harmony smiles in my doorway.

"Of course." My heart beats against my chest.

Harmony wraps her arms around me and I relax against her. I take in her sweet scent, something I've become more familiar with lately. It was a mix of lavender and lilac, which I think was in the shampoo she used. She kisses me, her lips melting against mine and I groan. Her tongue dips in my mouth and I suck on it gently.

"Wait, come in you'll let bugs in." I stop her, realizing we're kissing with door open.

"Sorry," she blushes and I pull her inside.

"I missed you." I admit.

The sides of her lips tilt up, "You did?"

"I did, and Millie too." I look down, avoiding eye contact with her.

"You did?" She tilts my chin with her thumb to look at her and she's smiling now.

"I just, thought it was nice having you both here." I shrug like it's no big deal. I don't think I could handle it being a big deal.

"Jamie was surprised I introduced Millie to you." She says.

"Was she upset?" The last thing I wanted was to start drama with Millie's other mom.

"No, just surprised because it's not something I've ever done."

"Oh."

"Yeah."

Harmony and I are both quiet while her words sink in. Was I special enough to her to introduce me to Millie, even if it was just as friends? I knew Harmony liked me, she'd made that clear. But the extent of how much hadn't settled in yet. Was she falling for me? I didn't think after Will I'd even date anyone again. I wasn't in the market for a relationship and yet here was a woman who literally showed up on my doorstep and became mine. My eyes begin to water and I try to blink the tears away but Harmony catches them.

"What's going on?"

I shake my head, unable to speak.

"I'm not going anywhere until we talk about it. Something is clearly going on." Harmony insists. She's not pushy, I know if I told her I didn't want to talk about it, she'd drop it. She was just concerned. It was the first time I've cried in front of her.

"I didn't expect to feel like this." I wipe my eyes and sniffle.

"Like what?" She furrows her brows in confusion.

"I really like you." I pause, trying to figure out the words. "I didn't think after ending an engagement, I was going to find anyone. Let alone someone so quickly. And then now there's you and *Millie*. And it terrifies me completely because the last time I started to like someone they turned out so differently than they were in the beginning. And I just never saw it until it was too late."

"I know you're scared because of what you went through, but I'm not him." She puts her hand in mine and rubs her thumb across the back of my hand.

"I know, and that's even scarier!" I exclaim.

Harmony laughs, a small chuckle before smiling. "They say the scarier things are, the more you are afraid of losing them."

"I just didn't expect to feel this. But I don't want to lose this feeling."

"What do you mean?"

"I want to be your girlfriend. I don't want someone else snatching you up when I'm busy thinking it over. There's nothing else to think over. I want you, and Millie in my life and I want to be yours and I don't want to share you with anyone. Well, except Millie."

"For real?" Her eyes widen.

"Yes."

"You know I wasn't looking for anyone else to be with right? Like you don't have to rush into this if you aren't ready."

"I know. I just can't imagine not feeling like this. I like missing you. I like being with you. I like spending time with you." I tell her.

"I like being with you too." She says softly.

"So be my freaking girlfriend already." I laugh.

"Well, I don't know. I think we're moving a little fast..." She teases and I roll my eyes at her. "Of course, I'd love to be your girlfriend."

I pull her body into mine, a warm hug and her lips find mine in an instant. I relax under her touch. She was mine and there was no going back. I mean sure, something could happen and maybe we'd break up. But right now, Harmony was mine. I couldn't dwell on the what ifs and the maybes when right now I knew how I felt.

"Why don't we go for a drive? I want to take you somewhere." Harmony suggests.

"Okay." I nod.

She gives me a few minutes to collect myself and change out of my pajamas. Harmony's waiting by the door when I come back. I'm not sure where we're going and while that would usually bother me, I was just happy to be with her. Harmony leads me to her car and takes my hand in hers while she drives. She's not using her GPS for once, so this place must be close. She wasn't totally familiar with all of Lovers without it yet.

"I found this by accident one night, and I thought you'd like it. Sometimes I come out here to watch the stars." Harmony explains as we pull up to an overlook.

It's a little out of the way, trees and stuff blocking behind us. But in front, the lighthouse is prevalent, and the sky is illuminated with an array of stars. I'm in awe of being able to see the sky so clearly, it looks like I could reach up and touch them if I wanted to. Harmony unlocks the car and walks around to my side. She stops to get a blanket out of the backseat and throws it over the front of her car. We both hoist ourselves on the hood and sit next to each other.

"This is beautiful." I smile at her.

"I really like you, Alana. I know this is all new for us, especially since you've never been with a woman before but I just want you to know I'm here no matter what pace you set. I'm yours until you tell me otherwise."

I take her hand in mine, rubbing my thumb on the back of her hand. "I feel the same."

"I know how unexpected this feels, but I almost feel like I was meant to know you."

"I'm starting to think that too." I admit.

Epilogue

1 YEAR LATER...

NORAH

"Have you seen Finley's blanket? I don't want her getting chilly." I call out to Gemma.

"It's June, babe." Gemma reminds me.

"Yes, but what if the temperature changes?"

Gemma laughs, "It's on the couch by the coffee table, I'll grab it."

As she steps out of the room, I finish changing Finley's diaper and button up her onesie. She gurgles sounds at me and looks at me with her bright green eyes. Her little red curls are pulled into two little pig tails on top of her head. She barely has any hair, just enough to get them sticking up.

"Good morning my love. Are you excited? We get to see your aunties today." I smile. She makes a face and shoves her hand in her mouth.

"Here we are, anything else?" Gemma's back with her blanket.

"I don't think so, I'm her food supply and we have the diapers packed."

"Hello pretty girl, you look just like your mama today don't you? So precious." Gemma smiles at Finley and I hand her over.

Gemma covers her in kisses like she does most mornings and Finley giggles. She loved Gemma almost as much as I did. She was only a few months old, but from the start Gemma had been there and she knew, just like I did that she loved her.

We tried to wait to move in together but it ultimately made more sense since Gemma was sleeping over most nights anyway. She helped with Finley more than I ever asked, giving me help through the sleepless nights and the joys of having a newborn. If you didn't know us, you'd assume Gemma was Finley's other mother. We were still taking things slow, not rushing the other things like marriage or anymore kids, but I loved having her around.

"I'm glad Ryleigh and Wrenn are back from the trip, I hope they didn't think I was crazy for making them fever check before we see them." I didn't want to be an overprotective mother, but I also didn't want something happening to her.

"No, it's a simple request. You love her, of course you're just keeping her safe." Gemma kisses my forehead.

"I wonder what Alana and Harmony wanted to tell us, she said it was important but wanted to tell everyone as a group."

"Well, maybe she found somewhere to live and they're moving out of the estate house." Gemma says.

"Hmm, maybe."

"Don't overthink it, I'm sure it's good news." Gemma smiles.

"Fine, let me have Finley so I can feed her before we go." I hold out my arms, and Gemma hands her to me.

WRENN

"Why did I think it would be a good idea to stay up all night and not get any sleep?" Ryleigh groans.

"Excuse me, I tried to get some sleep but someone wanted to have sex in a real bed." I remind her.

"Well, it's been so long." Ryleigh groans again.

"Come on, I'll make you some coffee. Go shower, we can't be late for the first get together since we've been gone."

"Fine. But can you bring me the coffee in the shower?"

"Okay." I laugh.

Heading to the kitchen, I'm glad it's stocked. Ryleigh and I have been traveling for most of the last year and there was only a handful of items we've picked up so far. Heather and Sage helped us move in last week when we got back, making sure Cheeto was back home too. We were mostly still packed up and I had a feeling it would stay like that for a bit. Because we were too busy seeing people and having sex to manage not to live out of boxes.

I make Ryleigh and I some coffee, bring it to her in the shower and join her. She takes a sip before putting it on the window sill out of the water. The water was nice and warm, and Ryleigh was all soaped up. The bubbles sticking to her every curve while I grabbed a washcloth for myself.

"I love you." I smile.

"I love you too." She kisses me softly and groans.

"No way, we do not have time for this. Alana will kill us if the first time she sees us in a year and we're late *again*."

"Fine, but later?" Her eyes twinkle.

"Yes, later on I'll bend you over every surface and make you forget your name. I promise."

We both get cleaned up, dressed and I feed Cheeto before we go. Ryleigh's playing with her engagement ring again, something I've noticed her doing whenever she's anxious.

"Are you okay?"

"Just nervous, we haven't told anyone yet."

"It's not like anyone will be surprised. We spent the last year traveling the world together. Everyone's going to be overjoyed."

"I'm just worried about Alana." She sighs.

"My sister is happy with Harmony now. I doubt she'll be upset we've decided to get married. Heather and Sage are getting married this summer, and she's not upset." I point out.

"That's true."

"Let's tell everyone so we can celebrate and start planning a wedding together." I smile.

"Only if you promise not to be a runaway bride." She teases.

"I promise." Sealing my promise with a kiss.

KIM

"Wait, what?" Zara looks at me, her jaw dropping on FaceTime.

"I applied for the charter school in NYC and I got the permanent teaching position." I say with a smile. I was a little more nervous than I was letting on, it was the most bold thing I've ever done when it came to love. I'd have to move out of Lovers and to NYC and I was doing it for me, but I was also doing it a lot for her.

"Oh my goodness! I didn't even know you applied!" She had sent me the application months ago, but I didn't say one thing about it. I was afraid to get my hopes up but now it was really happening.

"I wanted to surprise you." I smile.

"When do you come down?"

"My first day is September 5th so I need to have time to find a place and get settled."

"Move in with me!" Zara says like it's no big deal.

"What?" We'd done long distance the last year, and while it sucked and I missed her, it worked for us. It gave us the time to get to know each other better before we could make steps like this.

"Move in with me! You need a place and my roommate is moving out at the end of the month. Plus, having you in the city? It seems like the perfect chance for this."

"Okay."

"Okay?"

"Yes. I want to move in with you. I love you and I've loved the past year together but I'm ready to make some radical changes." I say.

"I cannot believe this! I'm so excited right now I'm literally buzzing." She smiles.

"I couldn't wait to tell you in person, but now I wish I had so I could kiss you."

"We'll see each other next weekend and we can start talking about things for the apartment. I can show you where the school is from my apartment and we can plan things out. I'm so freaking excited."

"Holy crap! I forgot to ask, did you hear about the book you sent to the publisher?"

Zara had gotten an agent and sent a book proposal to an agent looking for the type of books she writes. They were supposed to get back to her this week about moving forward with a contract or not.

"Yes! They offered me six figures to write the series! This is like the best day ever!" She smiles.

"We are most definitely celebrating when I get there. A fancy dinner for two and maybe a night at a hotel or something." I suggest.

"That sounds perfect for me!"

"You're perfect for me."

HEATHER

"Babe, Maeve's here!" Sage calls as I finish putting on my heels.

"Hey Maeve!" I call out.

We were all headed to Alana and Harmony's new place together so it made sense to car pool. We might not be drinking since Harmony's sober, but it was good for the environment.

"Have you seen my..." Sage is talking when I get down on one knee and hold open the red box.

"Sage Brooks—"

"Heather, are you..."

"Are y'all coming—" Maeve stops in the doorway and gasps. She immediately pulls out her phone and starts recording.

"I've been trying to catch you by surprise, which you can obviously see is difficult. But Sage Brooks, will you do me the honor of marrying me? You are the love of my life, someone I didn't expect to fall for and I thank heavens every day I did. I can't imagine not being married to you. Will you please be mine, forever?" I pop open the box, exposing a thin Black diamond band. I knew she didn't want a diamond ring like I had, that wasn't her style.

"Yes, oh my god." Sage bends down to kiss me, her lips melting into mine.

Then I slip the ring on her left hand and Maeve is crying behind us.

"I'm sorry! I swear they're happy tears!" Maeve gushes and we both laugh.

"You didn't have to do this, I already proposed." Sage says.

"I know, but I didn't want you walking around without a ring. Someone might try to snatch you up. And every woman deserves a proposal babe."

We both stand and Maeve excuses herself to wipe her eyes but I know she's giving us a moment alone.

"I really love you, and I just wanted to surprise you with this. I have only one request for the wedding." I say.

"Which is?" She raises an eyebrow.

"Can we take photos at the lighthouse? Even if it's just engagement photos or something."

"Of freaking course, I've already been trying to find a

photographer. I'm pissed I can't take them myself since I'll be in them." I laugh.

"We'll have to find someone who does them in your style."

ALANA

"Why do you look so nervous?" Millie asks me. She was way too smart for her age.

"I'm just anxious about springing a wedding on everyone." I admit.

"Mama said that too," Millie is in a pink floral dress with sparkles all over it. "But everyone loves weddings, and everyone whose coming loves you both. So why would they be upset?"

She's got me there. Before I can answer, I hear Harmony at the door.

"Can you give us a minute, Mills?" Harmony stands in the doorway in an all white suit.

"Sure mama," She waves goodbye to me and skips into the other room.

"I thought you might be nervous and I wanted to make sure there were no runaway brides around." Harmony says with a chuckle. She's the only one I'd allow to make jokes about that.

"Very funny. I just don't want anyone to be mad I didn't tell them."

"No, it's a small and intimate ceremony. Only our closest friends and family are coming. And considering your last attempt down the aisle, I think they'll be okay." Harmony reminds me.

"You're not nervous?"

"A little nervous about being married again, yes. But not nervous about you, no. I've been sure of this since the day we met." Harmony wraps her arms around me and I relax.

I inhale her sweet scent, and she rubs my back gently. I was wearing a white sundress, I had refused to go wedding dress shopping again. It was too much of a commotion and the last thing I wanted was to be in one and have a panic attack on my wedding day. We both agreed we'd done the big wedding thing, it was time to have a small intimate ceremony.

"Everyone will be here soon, why don't we take a little walk around back and check things out? I'm sure that'll make you feel better."

I smile, Harmony knew me better than I knew myself sometimes. She knew exactly what I wanted and how I was feeling. I've already checked on everything in our backyard, but I was happy to check again. Just in case. I was sure of Harmony, of this day no matter how unexpected it was.

Also by Shannon O'Connor

SEASONS OF SEASIDE SERIES

(each book can be read as a standalone)

Only for the Summer

Only for Convenience

Only for the Holidays

Only to Save You

Seasons of Seaside: The Complete Collection

LIGHTHOUSE LOVERS

Tour of Love

Hate to Love You

To Be Loved

Inn Love

Love, Unexpected

BEHIND THE SCENES SERIES

Eras of Us

Not My Fault

ETERNAL PORT VALLEY SERIES

Unexpected Departure

Unexpected Days

Eternal Port Valley: The Complete Collection

STANDALONES

Electric Love

Butterflies in Paris

All's Fair in Love & Vegas

Fumbling into You

Doll Face

Poolside Love

THE HOLIDAYS WITH YOU
(each book can be read as a standalone)

I Saw Mommy Kissing the Nanny

Lucky to be Yours

The Only Reason

Ugly Sweater Christmas

EVERGREEN VALLEY SERIES

How the B*tch Stole Christmas

POETRY

For Always

Holding on to Nothing

Say it Everyday

Midnights in a Mustang

Five More Minutes

When Lust Was Enough

Isolation

All of Me

Lost Moments

Cosmic

Goodbye Lovers

About the Author

Shannon O'Connor is a twenty something, bisexual, self published author of several poetry books and counting. She released her debut contemporary romance novel, *Electric Love* in 2021. O'Connor is continuously working on new poetry projects, book reviews, and more, while also diving into motherhood. When she's not reading or writing she can be found watching Disney movies with her son where they reside in New York. She is currently a full time mom and full time author.

She sometimes writes as S O'Connor for MF romances and as Shannon Renee for Poly romances.

Heat. Heart. & HEA's.

Check out more work & updates on:
Facebook Group: https://www.facebook.com/groups/shanssquad

Website: https://shanoconnor.com

- facebook.com/AuthorShanOConnor
- instagram.com/authorshannonoconnor
- bookbub.com/authors/shannon-o-connor
- pinterest.com/Shannonoconnor1498
- threads.net/@authorshannonoconnor

Printed in Great Britain
by Amazon